Title Page

Foreword

Next Year

Last Time Home

Ander's Family Forced Out

Railroading West

Welcome Homesteaders

Cutting and Burning

Neighbors

Coal Vein

Spice, Coal, and School

Winter Celebration

New Babies

A New Bride

Looking for Love

The Farmer takes a Wife

Another Bachelor Bites the Dust

Manfred Chooses a Bride

Bountiful Harvest

Harold gets a Daughter-in-Law

Life Goes On

Dedication

About the Author

Title Page

HOMESTEADERS HOPES

Taming the Wild Prairie

by Larry Odin Opseth

Foreword

One of our favorite songs growing up on the Great Plains was "Home on the Range". We all sang it in school, community meetings, and even in church. The old settlers who'd cut the sod for the first time, bachelor farmers, the town's people, our folks, and us kids all sang that song. We didn't have to look at any songbook for the words because we knew them by heart. Not only that, we believed them. It was our anthem on the prairie.

> Oh, give me a home
> Where the buffalo roam
> Where the deer and the antelope play
> Where seldom is heard
> A discouraging word
> And the skies are not cloudy all day

By the time we grew up on the farm there, most of the early homesteaders were gone. Some failed, some died, some sold out, but some hung on through good times and bad. Those that could, survived the loneliness, prairie fires, grasshoppers, the Great Depression, dust storms, and drought of the Dirty Thirties.

It was a hard life to be sure, but for those who yearned to own their own land, be their own boss, and raise up a family, it was a good life. There was plenty of loss to endure but the hardy persevered and passed on their hardworking ideals to their children.

This is such a story. Based on the lives of our family, neighbors, and friends in the flat Great Plains we grew up on.

NEXT YEAR

by Walter Allen "Bub" Owings
Editor of Burke County Tribune, North Dakota 1939
with permission of his son, Richard L. Owings 3-9-2017

We've farmed ten years for the next year,
We've died in the drifting soil,
We've seen the hoppers gobble
What we thought was ours for toil.
We've scraped up hay by the handful
And we've fed it by the spear,
We've shipped out all our cattle,
Watched our neighbors disappear.
We've prayed and toiled and struggled,
We've lived off Uncle Sam.
We've stole from him who fed us,
And we didn't give a damn.
Today our prayers have been answered
And we shout for all to hear:
Yes, we farmed ten years for nothing,
But we finally reached next year.

CHAPTER 1
Last Time Home

Sarah shivered as her eastbound train clickity-clacked through a frigid North Dakota white-out blizzard passing near their old failed homestead. The five-day journey from Oregon to Iowa gave her plenty of time to reminisce on how her seventy years had unfolded. Two thousand miles of America's landscape slid past the train windows displaying the places of her life in reverse. From their most recent meager decades in the Pacific Northwest, their long haul west through the mountains after hardworking decades homesteading the prairie grasslands, and finally, all the way back to the lush Iowa farmland of her youth.

Her life's events flickered through her mind like movie scene snippets. She thought of how the first promising, fertile homestead fields of waving grain were followed by the Dirty Thirties drought and grasshoppers causing their failure during the Great Depression. To her surprise, the farms had thrived again since she and Anders had left.

As her last day of rail travel came to an end, she was warmed by the memories of her younger life. She was home but Mother was gone and nothing would ever be the same again.

This was not the life she had imagined for herself.

#

Two days later, a trio of white-haired grannies strolled arm-in-arm on the downtown winter sidewalks of 1960 Woburn, Iowa, talking excitedly and even laughing some. At a glance, you could tell the three were sisters: Thelma the eldest, Mathilda the youngest, and Sarah, who was home for the first time in half-a-century for the funeral of their ninety-five-year-old mother.

Dressed in their going-to-church clothes under heavy coats, headscarves, and galoshes, they toured the town or at least as much as a bunch of grannies could handle in the winter. Sarah wore her sister's winter coat because she hadn't lived in a cold climate for decades. Even though it was cold enough to see their breath, thick mittens and mufflers pulled tight about their necks kept away the chill and light December snow.

Sarah was not bashful about gawking at the changes to the town as Thelma and Mathilda pointed out the old and the new. Memories of family and friends brought smiles. They had shed most of their tears the day before at the funeral of their dear mother Elsa who, despite a hardworking life, had outlived eight of her twelve children.

"Hang onto me, Sarah, you West Coast people don't know how to walk on snow anymore," Mathilda said with a smile.

"I'd forgotten how beautiful Christmas decorations are in the sparkling snow! Portland's weather is mostly wet and foggy. This is what Christmas should look like."

"The store lights are on because they stay open late until Christmas Eve," Thelma added.

"It's such a shame Mother couldn't have lived a few more weeks. She loved Christmas so much. *God Jul og en gledlige Nyte Orr* (good Christmas and a happy New Year) was how she always signed her Christmas letter to me," Sarah said with a soft smile. "She always wrote of the pretty snowflakes and the beautiful Jul tree in our old church out by the farm and the little kids singing carols for all they were worth."

"We can be sure Mother was looking down from Heaven, pleased that we had Christmas wreaths at her funeral and that the choir sang 'Silent Night' for her one more time," Thelma said. "Of course Mom actually liked 'Jingle Bells' best, but the old pastor wouldn't let them sing such a lively tune at a funeral."

"Such a shame. Mother would have told that minister it was her funeral not his," Mathilda laughed. "She wasn't afraid to tell any man what she thought. No wonder she never married again after Father died."

"I don't remember Father except for his picture on the wall," Sarah said. "I was only three when he passed away. Mother was a widow a long time. Apparently one husband was more than enough for her."

"She saw a lot of changes in her ninety-five years," Thelma said. "She was fifty before she saw an airplane fly over Woburn or even talked on a telephone when she lived in town with Nichola. My goodness but things have changed so much."

Mathilda said, "I think we had a Model T before any others. Harry was the first boy in our family to buy a car. He bought his before going out west to start ranching. That must have been 1909 or so."

"I wish he had stayed a few more days," Thelma said. "But he had to get back to his cattle. They're real cowboys out there, wild horses, range cattle, and the toughest pastureland in the world. Lots of rocks and prickly pear cactus is what his wife Ethel tells me. She would've stayed longer but they had train tickets. He isn't one to waste money. Harry's a tough old coot who'd wrestle a wild cat for a nickel." They all laughed. They loved their brother despite his stubbornness. Frugality saved his ranch even through the Depression and the Dirty Thirties.

#

As they strolled by the store windows, they enjoyed the light displays and gleaming gifts. The music store was broadcasting Christmas carols out into the street. Thelma laughed and remarked how their mother didn't think much of "Rocking Around the Christmas Tree". "Vat hass it got to do vit Christmas anyhow?" Thelma mimicked her mother's heavy Norwegian accent as her sisters burst out laughing.

"Ya, but she loved Burl Ives' 'Holly Jolly Christmas' song which doesn't even make sense to me," Mathilda chortled.

Mathilda started singing along with "Blue Christmas" on the loudspeaker. The other two chimed in and when it was done, Sarah said, "Mother really liked Elvis's songs. She even liked 'Hound Dog'. But after she saw Elvis gyrating on the Ed Sullivan Show that was it for her! No more Elvis."

"She did like a good movie now and then," Mathilda said. "To her, seeing the 'Ten Commandments' was better than going to church. She told everybody they had to see it."

"I hope God looks like Charlton Heston because she was sure that he was created in God's image himself," Sarah giggled. "Maybe she'd have married Charlton Heston if he'd come around and if he spoke Norwegian."

Their conversation paused as they traversed up the steep sidewalk to the church. They had been told that the Luther League mothers were having a lutefisk and lefse dinner. They still loved the old Norwegian traditional holiday foods which always seemed to taste better when served in a church basement. Besides that, after eating they only had to go upstairs to attend the evening Christmas services.

They sat in pews upstairs waiting to be called for seating because the basement dining room could only hold so many people. They usually served about five hundred at the annual event, a big fundraiser for the church because the food was donated by church members.

While waiting, many old friends and shirttail relatives came to them with condolences or just to see Sarah after such a long absence. It was heartwarming for her, she had sorely missed the close friends and tight-knit family. *Maybe being an old maid here wouldn't have been so bad.* Thoughts of her children and grandchildren that she would never have had made her shake that thought away.

#

The three of them were amused overhearing a young Woburn woman in the next pew trying to explain to her fiancé just what they were going to eat and why it was so special. "Okay, but what is lefse and what is lutefisk and why does everybody keep saying uffda," the young man with the harsh East Coast accent said a bit too loudly.

"Lefse is the traditional Norwegian soft flat bread made of potatoes. It looks kind of like a giant, soft, tortilla. We butter it, sprinkle on sugar, roll it up like a tight tortilla, and eat it with coffee or dinner. It's a special treat for us at holidays.

"Lutefisk is a little harder to explain. My family is split on its edibility. It's a leftover tradition from the starving times in Norway in the 1800s. But even back then when there was no other food, the Norwegians caught lots of cod in the North Sea. Since they didn't have refrigeration, they hung the cod in the sun until it got dry and hard. They stacked it like boards to ship it. You could keep it for years before eating it. Since you can't eat hard-as-wood fish, it had to be soaked to make it soft enough to eat. To get rid of the bones and soften it, they put lye in the water with the fish. Oh for such a terrible smell it produces!

"Once the fish was softened up and the biggest bones and skin had dissolved for the most part, the meat was still flaky and solid. If you didn't let it sit in the lye water too long and turn it into fish Jell-O, it was ready to cook after you rinsed it with fresh water. At best, it's nice, flaky fish with melted butter.

"Add some boiled potatoes on the side and there you have a dinner bountiful enough to fill your belly. It was one of the rare foods that was cheap and plentiful for the general population of Scandinavia. It was celebrated because it meant full plates for all. As for myself, I never could get past the smell. I usually only eat the meatballs and lefse unless Grandma is there and then I have to pretend to love lutefisk. Uffda."

Her fiancé looked at her with a raised eyebrow so she explained, "Uffda is purely a Midwest Scandinavian term that is not quite cussing and not quite 'no comment'. It's the equivalent of Oy Vay for the Jewish. 'Uffda, now that is a funny story' or 'uffda, that is sure too bad your dog ran away with your wife'. 'Uffda! I ate too much, uffda'. There, that's as good as I can explain it. Just

11

try the food and act nice. Us Norwegians don't get real expressive."

Just then they called the young couple's number. The Larson sisters watched them go. He looked like he was sniffing the air for the smell of fishy lye. "Wonder if he'll like it or make a fool of himself. He doesn't know it but half of her relatives are sitting down there waiting to see what kind of a man she's brought home. There can't be a better test than eating lutefisk for the first time can there?" Sarah said. All three ladies and some others sitting close by chuckled at that.

They enjoyed the dinner immensely and then relaxed in a pew upstairs for the evening service and wonderful choir music. They were delighted with the children's choir and especially the men's choir who sang some traditional Norwegian favorites.

Sarah sat there thinking of how this week had unfolded from the scratchy, long-distance telephone call last week bearing the news that Mother had passed away. It was a call she had been expecting for the last two decades, but nevertheless, hard to accept when it came. She felt guilty for not being able to come home to see her mother while she was still living.

# # #

Reminiscing later over coffee at Mathilda's house, they talked about their mother moving in with their sister Nichola after leaving the farm, and how Nichola passed away during World War II, so

Mathilda took over Mother's care. The sisters talked about how adventurous a life Sarah must have lived, moving to the wild Great Plains and then to the Pacific Coast. Thelma piped up, "Mother said you would never have left except for those railroad-delivered love letters."

Sarah nodded and said, "That was back in 1910 when I still lived with her. Most women my age were already married. I was worried about being an old maid. After all, I was going on twenty! Those letters changed my life. If you remember, it all started when us kids went to summer Bible school at the country church just over the Minnesota border closer to Tranquil." It was common practice for little country churches to consolidate for a week-long Bible school. There were new kids there that summer which made it more interesting.

Mathilda added, "It was more fun learning religion at Bible school than sitting on cold, hard pews reciting from the scriptures in our country church. The young intern minister and Bible school teachers made sure we had plenty of games, picnics, and hikes celebrating God's nature. The streams and forests in the little valley were so pristine, they almost felt holy."

One of the new kids was Anders, one of the many Kross kids from Tranquil, Minnesota. Sarah had just finished second grade and he fifth grade. Anders was cute with curly blonde hair, full of fun and laughter. Sarah was a smiley, lively farm girl raised doing chores and helping her mother. She had white-blonde hair like her siblings. From the first day, Anders and Sarah had a crush on each other, walking around hand-in-hand whenever they could. Their week together went by much too fast. On the last day, they promised to see each other the following summer. There might even have been a quick hug between the two. He was her first boyfriend. The teachers thought it was sweet.

"There was never to be another Bible school together," Sarah said. "I was crestfallen when we arrived at Bible school the next summer and learned that Anders' father had moved the whole family to homestead somewhere in the Dakotas."

CHAPTER 2
Ander's Family Forced Out

The reason the Krosses moved was because Anders' father Harold needed a bigger farm than he was able to rent near Tranquil. With a pregnant wife and six kids already, it was just too tight financially. Renting the land and having to feed and clothe the family made it impossible to break even. Harold confessed to his wife Anna, "I'm getting tired of having nothing but a cash receipt at the end of every year."

When Harold's grandfather arrived from Norway fifty years earlier with his wife and six children, open land around there was plentiful. Harold's father was eighteen at the time. He soon married and claimed a good farm. Harold was born in 1865. Southern Minnesota had good farm land with trees, water, wild game, nice towns, roads, and railroads. It was a good place to live.

Banks were prosperous but that was part of the problem. Taking out any kind of loan from a bank was to risk losing it all. Interest on loans added up fast and if there was less than a bountiful crop, lots of defaults happened. Banks used sheriffs to evict defaulting farm families after all their personal possessions, and sometimes even their clothes, were auctioned off to pay down the debt.

Neighbors disappeared without notice. Sometimes they were seen heading away in their wagon with whatever they could carry or some were seen clambering onto outbound trains with only their trunks. Many escaped to bigger cities, some headed east or west for fishing or foresting jobs. There were a few who gave up on the American dream and took their families back to the old country in defeat. They had all set out with hopes of becoming rich in America and returning home wealthy. Failure was a bitter pill to swallow. Many of them had believed by coming to America they would become rich by picking up the gold they claimed was lying in the streets. Alas, it was not so.

#

During the 1899 summer of Bible school, Harold was seeing foreclosures happening to more neighbors. He was not optimistic about a future in southern Minnesota for himself and his family, but he did not want to move to a big city work in a factory. He had heard of the drudgery and preferred farming and being his own boss.

Harold and Anna read the news and advertisements in the Posten, an Iowa Norwegian language newspaper. They were intrigued by stories of free farmland out on the Great Plains. Filing for a quarter section was free with another quarter section if they planted trees on it, as long as they settled on the land for five years. Railroad ads promoted the move up to the *land of milk and honey,* where wheat grew straight up with hardly any effort, cattle grew fat on free buffalo grass, and rain followed the plow.

They even heard from relatives in Norway who had seen the railroad circulars and wildly exaggerated stories of free land in the newspapers. Europeans were practically starving, potato blight and droughts left the overcrowded countries with nothing to eat. Harold and Anna's ancestors had left the old country for the same reasons during an earlier potato blight. Even though Harold and Anna knew they should be thankful that their family was not starving, they chafed under the desire for a better life. They were stubborn and proud, yearning to be their own landlords, owners of their own destiny. When they were in town, they had many discussions with other young farm renters like themselves. They saw the steady stream of families heading west to settle on homestead claims.

While the kids were in Bible school, Harold learned their farm rent was going up again. After fall harvest, he settled up with the landlord, giving him most of their year's earnings. He quietly visited the land office to see what western homestead land was available. He had a good eye looking at maps and the clues on them. If they were going to go homesteading out west, now was the time before all the good farmland was claimed. There were claims available in northern Minnesota but it looked to be all forest peat bog land. The rich land of the Red River Valley in North Dakota had already been claimed.

By the time the kids were out of Bible school, Harold had brought home a potential land claim and information from the railroad on costs to move up to the station closest to the best-looking land that he thought might work for them. He needed all of Anna's support if they decided to be homesteaders.

She ran the house while he did the farming and livestock. She was a strong woman and obviously fertile because they had a new baby every couple of years. That was a blessing for him but a lot of weariness and work for her. She knew she was going to have another one coming in late winter. If they moved to the middle of the buffalo grass plains, she would not have the support of her mother, sisters, and aunts when the baby came.

Together they wrote lists of everything they might need, adding and re-adding the costs. They wanted two quarters of land but would have to come up with enough money for materials to build a house, barn, and the rest of a farm. They'd take along their farm equipment and at least one strong horse team, pigs, chickens, and milk cows. They had no illusions that they would need stout beasts and sturdy plows along with their strong backs if they had a chance of surviving and thriving up there, even though isolated from their families. No matter how many times they added up the numbers, they did not have enough to move, build, plant, and eat until selling their first wheat crop. They didn't have enough cash to make the move even after selling some of their stock and less valued possessions.

That was when Anna brought out her secret tin box filled with enough money to pay the rest of the railroad transportation. Harold was flabbergasted but relieved beyond expression. All their married years, frugal Anna had been slipping small amounts of cash into her secret posthole bank. It was just pennies and quarters here and there as well as the odd birthday gift, but she kept it to herself. The little tin box was at the bottom of the loose fence post at the corner where the blackberry bush grew. It was Anna's secret and she guarded it wisely for the ultimate emergency.

With a hug and a tear in his eye, Harold said, "Dear wife, you've given us the miracle we need to get us out of here. Thank you, and thank God!"

#

With that, they decided that they were going to leave as soon as they could this fall. The rest of the summer and fall was busier than usual. Every family member big enough to walk was put to work gathering garden produce and picking wild berries. Anna pickled the produce, made cabbage into sauerkraut, and dried beef and fruit in greater quantities than usual. Everything they didn't need to consume immediately was packed into baskets in their root cellar. They had wonderful squash and pumpkins that year. Every ounce of extra milk was turned into cheese. Harold hunted every deer, duck, and goose they could get to fatten their larders.

Anna's sisters and nieces helped sort and pack everything from the rented farmhouse that they would need on the prairie frontier. Her grandmother kept saying, "Ve come from da old country with only two suitcases and one immigrant trunk in the bottom of that terrible ship." When she saw the stacks of clothes and utensils that Anna and girls were sorting through, she said, "Where you think you are going? It's not the moon, it's just North Dakota!"

Anna would smile and nod her head, "Yes, Gramma, you're right but I'd rather take it with if I can, rather than have to make it again or buy it up there." With a slight grimace she added, "We don't have enough cash to live on much less buy everything new again. We'll have to make do." Many times over the following years she thought Gramma was right, it was North Dakota not the moon, but it felt further away than the moon sometimes.

#

Every bit of clothing was sorted, patched, and washed. Items that were too worn were given to others to use as rags or they were made into quilts or rag rugs. There was no room or money to ship rags or frivolous items. She left her wedding dress and fancy shoes for her nieces to use someday. Hard decisions were made about what cookware and sewing supplies to take.

Her beautiful old spinning wheel went to a niece because she had not used it for years and there were no sheep coming with to get wool from anyhow. She knew she could order cloth from the Sears catalog. All their shoes were examined and those needing repair or new soles were taken to their cousin the shoemaker. Kids and some adults spent much of the summer barefooted to save on shoes, but up on the rough frontier they might have to wear shoes and boots most of the time.

Harold's uncle came over with a surprise going away gift. "Here ya go ya young whippersnapper," he said gruffly. "Them ducks and geese'll be flying higher up there so this old 10-gauge double-barreled shotgun will surely knock 'em down. At least you'll be able to eat and you can use slugs to get them deer, too."

Harold was overwhelmed with gratitude to get a good shotgun because all he had was an old single-shot 20-gauge that was good for small birds and ducks. He had his little .22 single-shot bolt action rifle that was good for shooting rabbits and skunks. "This will be real handy up there. I'll use it well. I'm a pretty good shot so I won't be wasting shells," he said with a wink.

"Ya, them new smokeless shells is more'n two cents nowadays. So here's what I got left for it." He handed Harold a canvas bag bulging with shotgun shells. "There's slugs and double-aught and bird shot. Some of 'em are old black powder so you have to shoot closer with those." He smiled as he handed over the bag. "This old shotgun's a strong one and won't blow up on you."

Harold smiled his thanks for this valuable and thoughtful gift. "Don't you worry, I'll only shoot at ducks that fly low so I don't put too much of a strain on the barrels." They both laughed. "Good thing those big old buffalo aren't up there any more or I'd have to have an army rifle."

"Ya, sure, and the Indians have been moved to reservations, too. That Minnesota Indian war and then Custer's massacre are done with. Else you couldn't take Anna and the kids up there. Her Granny woulda thumped you with that rolling pin of hers." They both laughed at that because Gramma was known to be pretty owly now and then. More than one salesman had lumps on their heads from trying to cheat that old lady. "She's nearsighted but no fool," his uncle guffawed.

"Lucky for me Anna didn't inherit that ornery trait. She must've got the steadfast trait from the other side of the family."

Uncle nodded his head in total agreement and said, "Harold boy, you're a strong young man. You got a good wife and strong, healthy children. You'll do good up in Nort' Dakota. Now I got a favor to ask of ya. My boy Oskar'd like to go up there with you. He wants to see if he should take up a claim but don't want to spend the filing fee yet."

Harold nodded with a serious expression on his face. "I could use another man to help me get set up this fall."

"He's twenty now. Knows his farming and is strong as a young ox. I raised him right so he'd be a good helper."

"We'd be mighty thankful for his help. Anna will be pleased, she likes him and the kids think he's great."

"Tell him what he needs to pack. We'll send food for him, he has his own ax and tools. Good ox driver, too." The men shook hands as his uncle said, "I gotta get going home to get the cows milked before Auntie starts hollering." Harold knew Auntie took after Gramma with the loud voice and no qualms about saying what she thought.

#

There was a farm auction for one of the Quaker families moving back east and Harold got a nice cast iron kitchen range for eleven dollars. It burned coal or wood and had an oven and a water tank. They were thrilled because the stove they were using belonged to the rental farm they were on. Anna surprised him when she bid and got a treadle sewing machine for five dollars.

She was right proud of those two purchases. She had been looking in the Sears catalog and at the hardware store in Tranquil and knew how much they would cost new. She was thrilled that she would be able to sew and mend clothes faster and have an even better stove. She would soon find out how important that stove would be in the harsh Great Plains winter. Harold was happy because she was happy and even more so when she pulled the bid money out of her own apron pocket.

As the days drew nearer to the time to load everything on the train, more and more neighbors and relatives came to say goodbye. Some brought going away gifts but most had only well wishes and promises of keeping in touch by mail. Some gifts were funny and some were serious. They were given four fly swatters, some for the bugs, and some for the kids, and an old army compass so they could find their way out of the tall prairie grass.

Auntie came carrying two moth-eaten, heavy, woolen army topcoats. "These was Uncle's from back when him and them Norwegian boys was fighting the southerners in the Civil War." Anna's eyes welled with tears, not with emotion but from the strong smell of mothballs. "They're old but warm and big enough to be blankets on the beds. Ain't nothing to look at but you take them anyhow. Old but good," Auntie said firmly.

Anna knew there was no turning them down. Maybe we can throw them in the cattle car to air out. The smell might keep the flies away. When she showed them to Harold, he looked less than enthusiastic but agreed they were stuck with them. He wasn't about to get on Auntie's bad side either. Another cousin offered his father's old war sword but understood they couldn't take everything, so Harold persuaded him to keep it to give to his

24

grandchildren someday. That was one of the easier gifts to turn down.

"If we get much more stuff, we'll have to rent another boxcar," Anna remarked. They both knew that couldn't happen. They needed all the room they had to take all the containers and bags of produce, seed, and food for a year. They wouldn't have anything to harvest until next year. All their time this fall would be spent building a house and some kind of barn. It was going to be a tough time and they had no illusions of the importance of being as prepared as possible. They took as much food as they could carry.

Their last Sunday in Minnesota was spent at the country church where everyone brought something for a potluck dinner. As always, there was lots of food plus many prayers offered for them by the old preacher. They shared memories, laughter, and tears. The kids had a grand time playing with all their friends and cousins. They didn't know it would be the last time. They had been told they were moving but did not fully understand what it would entail. In those days, there was not a lot of need to explain anything to kids. Kids did what they were told, when they were told, and they didn't talk back.

The father was the undisputed boss of the farm, and the mother in charge of the house. It had always been like that and that's the way it would stay. The grandparents felt they were being deprived of the joy of their grandchildren but understood they had to let them go for the promise of a better future, just like their own grandparents in Norway had let them go fifty years ago.

The church ladies had made a large batch of rye crisp and crisp thin bread. These were both traditional breads that would keep for years. It was food they could rely on and if necessary, survive on it. Two of Anna's aunts proudly gave them a twenty-five-pound box of dried lutefisk. Harold and Anna both loved lutefisk even though some of the kids didn't. It was an acquired taste.

CHAPTER 3
Railroading West

Harold's brothers had a good cost saving idea. They all had extra sawn timbers and board lumber on their farms. The transport rental of a flatcar was cheaper than a boxcar so they built lumber boxes to hold everything. They even prebuilt sections of lumber walls and roof panels. They would use the lumber panels to construct buildings on the homestead. The cattle and horse shipping rates were a happy surprise. When they were ready to load up, dozens of relatives and friends came to load and build the walls and roof flats on the flatcar. Everything was secured with ropes tied to the flatcar cleats.

The cattle car was the last to be loaded with their two cows, work horses, pigs, chicken cages, and a strong young ox broken to the yoke. The cows resisted going up the chute. Oskar and Harold had to twist their tails to move them forward. It was how farmers dealt with livestock sometimes, not gentle but not cruel either. The ox was fresh meat on the hoof if they needed it and a work animal they could always use if they didn't have to eat it the first year.

The railroad did not charge for attendants of animals so Harold, Oskar, the two older boys Anders and Johan, and the oldest girl Lily rode with the animals as stock tenders with their dog Blondie and two cats. They brought the mothball-stinking army coats and hung them from the ceiling at the back of the car where the animals were tethered. Their eyes watered at first but they gradually got used to it.

The train had to stop for water and coal for the engines every few hours. They brought buckets so they could have drinking water and water for the stock at the rail stops. They stuck a chamber pot back in the corner just in case. The mothballs helped disguise the odor. They loaded hay for animal feed and extra straw and quilts to sleep on during the trip.

Anna, six-year-old Kersta, four-year-old Helene, and two-year-old Charles rode in the comfortless passenger car. There was no charge for babes in arms. Anna was not far enough along to restrict her ability to care for them by herself. Her sisters and aunts trooped into the railroad car carrying baskets of food, blankets, and pillows for her because she would be on her own except for whistle stops along the way when she and Harold might see each other for a few minutes.

The conductor didn't necessarily think that all three children were considered babes in arm, or that eight animals and a dog needed five stock tenders, but after he talked to the Tranquil ticket agent who was a friend of the family, he punched their tickets and it went well from there.

# # #

They had tickets all the way through to the rail siding closest to their homestead on the map. They didn't have to change train cars because the railroads switched their two cars and the passenger carriage from the short line in Minneapolis to the Soo Line for the remainder of the trip.

They had never been on train trip this long. It swayed, jerked, stopped, and started again and again. The clickity-clack of the wheels on the rails and the creaking sway of the train cars was bothersome at first but they gradually noticed it less and less. The locomotive engineer tooted the steam whistle at every crossing and every depot water stop. It was their first experience with motion sickness, but eventually it subsided.

Later that day they arrived in Minneapolis. They endured the next day and night on the move in the crowded passenger car and cattle car lit by smoky coal oil lamps, then another long day to Minot, North Dakota. Entertaining the little ones, feeding them, and keeping them from crying wore Anna out. There wasn't much for young, active children to do other than watch the plains of North Dakota glide by the windows. It looked the same in every direction.

The adults were stunned at the lack of trees and the absence of towns or farms the further west they went. It was open country without roads or even trails from what they could see. It took part of the next night to get to their Northfield railway siding. Just as dawn was breaking, they got off the train as their cattle and flatcars were shunted onto the siding. They watched railroad workers unload their livestock into the stockyard.

Harold paid two workmen to help dismantle and unload the wall panels, barrels, and crates from the flatcar. Meanwhile Oskar, Anders, and Johan assembled their wagon and got the horse harnesses ready. Luckily there had been no rain for the trip so everything came through with only some dust. The old army coats aired out pretty well in the cattle car with the wind whistling through day and night. They had to use them to keep warm and either they were getting used to the smell or the odor was going away. They joked about the yardman in Minneapolis who stuck his head in the cattle car door and exclaimed, "Holy cow, smells like my grandmother's closet!" They heard something like that quite a few times during their trek.

#

The Northfield railroad siding was bustling. There were a few new wood buildings lining dirt streets and even a few houses. Harold heard the clang, clang, clang of hammer on anvil so there had to be a blacksmith shop which he would need sometime. There were two new, unpainted churches, one with a steeple. Many of the town's people walked by watching them get off the train and to see whatever goods the train was unloading.

Harold saw men loading bushel bags into nearby boxcars. He asked them what they were shipping. Ready to brag a little, they were happy to tell him it was the wheat they had just harvested and sold to a mill in Minneapolis. He didn't ask but one of them said, "We're getting fifty-one cents a bushel but the railroad charges a nickel a bushel to ship it. We have over a hundred bushels to ship today and there's more coming in soon."

Two more farm wagons pulled up to the other boxcar and started to load bushel bags into it. It sounded like they were speaking some sort of Norwegian. Harold approached them saying, *"God daggen, vor de stor de til, er du Norske* (good day, how are you, are you Norwegians)?" They looked at him curiously and answered in a Norwegian dialect he barely understood. "I'm Harold Kross from Tranquil, Minnesota. Just came in on the train."

"You should go back there and bring heavier coats," one of the younger men answered with a laugh. "Wish I could go back to Tromso and get the big fur coat I left there."

"How long have you been here," Harold asked politely while speaking his dialect slowly so they could understand.

The men looked at each other and smiled, "Almost two years ago when this was the end of the rail line. We had to build a sod house and live in it with the horses and or we would have froze like the cod we used to fish in the Arctic."

The tall, red-bearded brother about Harold's age added, "By golly we made it though and plowed up twenty-five acres to plant wheat that spring. This ground is good for wheat but the grasshoppers sure like it better than buffalo grass."

"What are grasshoppers?" Harold asked, and was mystified when they all laughed and said he'd find out soon enough.

"We threshed out more than three hundred bushels and used most of it for seed this spring and sold the rest," the blonde brother said. "Had to buy flour and bacon."

"We farm four miles south of here. Just us four brothers," the redhead said. He pointed to each as he said, "Ivar, Bernt, Karl, and me, Lars. We are Johnsons from Tromso in Norway. We each put in a claim and planted a hundred acres of wheat this year."

Harold was astounded. *Are these men pulling my leg about that much wheat? Making fun of me just off the train?*

#

"Hey there, Harold, did you bring a wife with you," Karl asked.

When Harold nodded, Ivar blurted out, "Did she bring any sisters with her? We'd sure like to meet some nice Norwegian girls."

"No, it's just Anna and our six children. The oldest is twelve but he and his brother can work as hard as men. My cousin Oskar is with us, too."

32

"Well, Harold, you are a smart man to bring a wife and kids with you because you sure can't find a wife up here. There has to be a hundred bachelor farmers for every woman who steps off the train nowadays," Lars said.

Harold was saved from having to reply as Anna came to see what was taking him so long. She had listened to the last bit with a smile on her face because she understood their dialect pretty well since her grandfather had come from northern Norway.

"This is my good wife, Anna." Each of the men jumped to the ground and took off their hats politely. "These are the Johnson brothers farming four miles south. Lars, Ivar, Karl, and the youngest is Bernt." They each smiled as they were introduced.

"Where is your farm then?" Lars asked hopefully.

Anna answered for them, "We are just unloading from the train, getting the wagon and horses harnessed so we can go out to see where our land is. We don't know yet."

Harold added, "The land agent map shows it about five miles north and east of here."

The Johnson boys looked disappointed in that. "Oh shucks," Ivar said. "Wished you were south like us. We'd like to sample a good wife's cooking for a change. Bernt makes oatmeal for every meal." They all laughed.

"You will have to come and have Sunday dinner with us sometime when we're settled in," Anna invited with a warm smile.

33

Such handsome and polite men. I'll have to telegraph my cousins and have those girls come up here to marry some of these fine Norwegian boys.

#

"Maybe we'll come up with our guns and help you clean out some of the wolves that think this country still belongs to them, Lars said. "They used to eat buffalo before the army and railroad killed them off. But now there are only deer, some quick as a blink antelope, and huge jackrabbits. The coyotes and foxes eat jackrabbits and gophers."

All four brothers solemnly nodded in agreement. "You'd better believe it, those big wolves will eat your horse and cows, even your dog, cat, and even you before you know it if you don't kill them first," Bernt said grimly.

Karl blurted, "Goddamned wolves are the worst because they're so big and smart."

Lars punched him in the shoulder and said sharply, "Watch your foul mouth. Doncha remember how to talk when there's a lady around?"

Karl turned beet red. Looking at the ground he said, "Sorry, didn't mean nothing bad ma'am."

"I've heard worse but I don't like rough talk around the children," Anna replied.

Bernt was anxious to add his two cents worth, "The county and state have a bounty on wolves so be sure to keep the hide of any you kill. Wolves can even live off gophers. These Nort' Dakota flickertail gophers are quick and wary. They sure like to eat our oats and wheat stalks before we can get it all scythed down. Some of our neighbors and friends have lost horses and oxen, their legs broken when they stepped into gopher holes."

"You're selling wheat already?" Anna asked. When they nodded, she added, "How many bushels to the acre does this ground give back anyhow?"

Looking quite proud of themselves, Karl said, "We got fourteen bushels to the acre even after the grasshoppers took some."

Harold was skeptical. "How much can a grasshopper eat?" The brothers roared with laughter. *Lying braggarts, one hundred acres at fourteen bushels an acre at forty-six cents a bushel is more than six hundred and forty dollars. Bullcrap! What kind of fools do they take us for?* He shook himself out of his thoughts and stepped back. "Boys, it's been nice meeting you but we need to go find our homestead now."

He took Anna's arm and turned back to where Oskar and the kids were hitching up the team and loading the wagon. As they walked, he said quietly, "These Dakota boys are sure big liars. Never heard such falderal in my whole life."

"Why is that? They looked and sounded like nice boys to me. They didn't cuss or take the Lord's name in vain except once." Maybe I better wait with sending that telegram to my cousins until I know them better.

#

Anna went to the railroad depot post office and mailed the letter to her mother that she had been writing on the train. She sent it off with a two-cent stamp so her family would know they arrived at their destination in good shape except for being tired and the kids having motion sickness the first day. Truth be told, she felt queasy part of the trip but maybe that was because of the pregnancy. She had to hurry back to make sure Harold and Oskar put the right supplies in the wagon for the first nights.

She made them fill the big barrel with fresh water after the depot agent said not to drink any water at the farm without boiling it first. The railroad had a good, fresh water well and allowed them to fill up from it. Julian, the depot agent, was proud of the brand-new steel tower with a high tank and an Aeromotor windmill. It was pumping water when the wind was blowing which seemed to be most of the time.

When they finished loading the wagon, Anna said, "Put those army coats on the back of the load. They still stink." The whole family stretched their legs for a quick walk around the brand-new dirt streets to see what was there and what was being built. They were impressed that the eight-block town would be bursting at the seams in no time.

They were anxious to set out that afternoon and find the surveyor stakes with their numbers on them. The wagon was full, so Oskar and the boys trotted alongside. They and Blondie, the collie, kept busy herding the cattle and pigs, who just wanted to stop and eat the tall grass and flowers every few steps. Their two farm cats were content to ride in the back of the wagon as they went down the rough, barely perceptible prairie trails.

The kids were having fun running and yelling after being cooped up in the train for almost three days. "You all keep track of each other. If you go into the tall grass we'll never find you again," Anna hollered, and she wasn't joking. There were all sorts of colorful butterflies and huge dragonflies as well as small, bright-green grasshoppers, and enormous brown grasshoppers that jumped and flew through the air with a fluttery buzz. They heard meadowlarks singing all around and saw more red-winged blackbirds than they thought existed in the world.

Mosquitos rose out of the grass and descended on them. "These darn mosquitos sure are big and hungry," Anna said as she swatted at them. Harold and the boys weren't bothered too much because they had been in the fields all summer where there were always mosquitos. Anna covered up the girls as best she could. When a stiffer breeze came up from the east, the mosquitos were blown away, at least temporarily. Soon the littlest children were sleeping in Anna's arms and on the canvas in the back of the wagon.

They spotted four farmsteads off a mile or more from the trails they were trying to follow on the map. A few times they had to detour around sloughs with open water or cattail-filled muddy bogs. They were anxious to meet any neighbors there might be. They were used to having neighbors and it felt pretty empty out here. With the fresh breeze and the warm sun, it was a great day to be out exploring the prairie.

Blondie woofed in surprise when three big prairie chickens flew up almost underfoot as they marched down the trail. The large birds burst out of the grass with a loud whir before disappearing again. The horses startled and snorted so Harold had to pull tight on the reins. Black and silver geese and ducks flew over them almost every mile.

The girls were delighted by the wild flowers and small bushes of fragrant wild prairie roses that stood out of the prairie grass. Oskar said, "Where there are flowers, there are bees and honey. We'll find the hives and steal the honey." Three times whitetail deer bounded out in front of them only to vanish in the tall grass.

"Sure is a lot of meat on the hoof for the taking out here," Harold remarked with a smile.

On the wagon seat Anna asked, "Harold, why are they lying?"

"Who be lying to you already," Oskar asked.

"Oh," Harold sighed, "some farmers loading wheat bags on the train said they have a hundred acres of wheat harvested and the boys on the other boxcar said they were getting fifty-one cents a bushel but paying a nickel to ship it. If you add that up, that's more than six hundred and forty dollars this year. That's nonsense. Liars is what they are."

Anna pursed her lips doing the arithmetic in her head. "Yes, that would be the amount. But why would two different groups lie to you like that?"

Harold said he'd have to think about that and check it more with the depot agent. *We've never harvested that much wheat on our farm any year.*

They continued on the prairie trail reading claim stake numbers. It was hard to tell distances out here except that the posts were half-a-mile apart as set by the U.S. Army surveyors. The railroad had only been pushed this far into North Dakota two summers before.

The opportunity to own three hundred and twenty acres of good farmland free and clear was made possible by the American Homestead Act, and was just too good to pass up. Railroad companies had pressured Congress to open up more of the Great Plains to new settlers so they jumped at the chance when the rail lines and depot towns were complete enough to get settlers and farm equipment out there. Crops were railroaded east to flour mills in Minneapolis and eastern cities.

After a couple of hours of slowly bumping along the trails, Anders and Johan came running back hollering that they found their stake numbers just ahead. They stopped the wagon at the first stake and stood on top of the wagon to look at as much of it as they could. They were at the southwest corner of their two quarters. "There! To the north and east. That must be the stream and ponds that showed on the land agent's map," Harold exclaimed, pointing off in that direction. "But where are the trees? Don't streams have trees around them?"

Shading her eyes with her hand, Anna replied with a furrowed brow, "Well, we had read there were not a lot of trees out here."

"Yes, but I didn't know they meant there weren't any trees," Harold said softly back.

CHAPTER 4
Welcome Homesteaders

The entire family stood by the stake. "Welcome home everybody," Harold almost shouted with a big smile on his face. Anna smiled too, but maybe not quite as broadly. Oskar, Anders, and Johan looked at each other with raised eyebrows and little grins. The younger kids were totally confused.

"Where's our house, Mama?" Kersta, the six-year-old asked crossly. Four-year-old Helene started to cry, but Charles, the two-year-old, was oblivious.

"Everybody hold hands," Anna said enthusiastically to hide her own fears. She, Harold, and Oskar each took two children by the hand. "We're going to walk across our new land and see what's over at that creek. Let's see if there are any ducks over there." They started marching in a line looking closely at everything on the way. After a hundred yards, Charles wanted to be carried so Anna picked him up. Then the four-year-old wanted a piggy back ride so Harold lifted her up on his shoulders.

Sometimes the prairie grass was shoulder high, waving in the wind like beautiful ocean waves. Some grass was only knee high, thick and fibrous, but not very green. There were very few of what they considered to be weeds. A line of green grass and plants edged the creek but no trees or bushes. Sunflowers, tall feathered grasses, cattails, and wild flowers made it all feel surreally beautiful. The kids chased monarch butterflies and scads of white butterflies.

"The land agent says there are no rattlesnakes up here, at least we don't have to worry about poisonous snakes," Harold said. It was meant to be encouraging but it scared the girls and the younger boys.

"Maybe not, but there's a bunch of crows over there that have found something dead. Uffda!" Oskar said holding his nose.

When they got up to the creek area it was a disappointment. There was no babbling brook, at least not this time of year. The creek bottom or coulee as the farmers around there called it, was green. Some little pools called sloughs were in the creek bed with cattails around them. "If we could eat and sell cattails we'd be good," Anna said ruefully. Apparently, the creek was only filled in the spring time. It was more like a series of shallow ponds most of the time without fish, just the odd turtle and frogs that thrived there.

A half-mile by a whole mile of prime farmland seemed enormous to them after the smaller farms they were used to in southern Minnesota. Survey stakes with section numbers at half-mile spacing ran for hundreds and hundreds of miles. Every train coming into the frontier bore settlers anxious to get to their new land. Like Harold and Anna, hardly any of them had seen the land before filing their claims. All they had seen were lines on a map enhanced by hopeful imaginations.

Harold thought he was smart to claim the section with a creek running on one side of it. At least he would have open water for his cattle and horses but now knew there'd be no fish to catch. Ducks and geese should be easy to hunt here. The creek bottom would be good for haying and pasture but appeared too soggy for farming. It wasn't much to brag about and Harold tried to hide his disappointment from the others.

#

While the children frolicked under the wagon, Harold and Anna walked around deciding where to build the barn and house and where the grain fields and pastures should be. They stacked rocks at every corner of where they wanted things to be. Oskar and the older boys walked back to get the wagon and the animals. They picked a higher bump on the edge of the coulee to set up their big tent for the night and unloaded most of the stuff from the wagon.

Oskar and Harold set the heavy, cast iron stove on some flat rocks they'd pulled together so Anna could cook some oatmeal for supper with a big pot of coffee. They also had two or three days of bread, cheese, and sausages in Anna's train baskets. Anders milked the cows so the little kids were filled up for the night. They set up three bed frames and slept almost open to the stars under the quilts. The night cooled off surprisingly fast.

They soon discovered the mosquitos were out in full force and after some squealing and slapping, Anna spread a light cheesecloth over cribs and bedposts which helped keep the buzzing bugs away so they could sleep. But then the chirp, chirp, chirp of crickets started. It was one of those sounds that you couldn't ignore until you were just too exhausted to stay awake any more. Luckily the children fell asleep and did not wake up until morning. It had been an exciting but exhausting journey for them as well. Anna prayed silently for the strength and stamina to help Harold make this venture a success.

#

Birds woke them way too early with their loud singing. They wanted to sleep some more but soon everyone was awake and then more rest was impossible. Harold and Anna realized that long hard days of work lay ahead of them and the sooner they got started, the better.

At midmorning, Harold and the two older boys drove the wagon back into town and loaded up as much as they could to take out to the homestead along with another barrel of water. Julian, the depot agent, said not to worry about the safety of their boxes sitting there. Nobody was stealing anything from his rail yard. Just the same, they took three wagonloads out to the homestead.

They soon discovered one of the difficulties out here was trying to get kids to go to bed at a reasonable time because they were so far west and north that sundown didn't occur until ten o'clock and bright twilight lasted another hour. The kids wanted to keep running around playing because it wasn't dark yet. They played kick-the-can, hide-and-seek, and tag. Anna's only rule was all the kids had to stay in the farmyard. The boogey man was still real back then.

The next day they brought out two more loads of their storage boxes and sacks. They had a harder time figuring how to move the wall and roof panels. Julian said to stack them in the back corner of the railyard for as long as they wanted. They put down sleepers to keep the wood panels off the ground until they could come back and get them.

#

On the second evening on their Northfield homestead, a young, sunburned, blonde man rode up on a work horse. He greeted them in a language they could not understand. They finally understood from the few English words the man could speak that he was a German bachelor farmer from a half mile west and a mile north of them. Some German and Norwegian words were the same so that helped a little. He had seen the smoke from their stove. Mostly they did a lot of smiling, shaking hands, and nodding while trying to make a friend out of their first neighbor. Anna offered coffee and some of her big oatmeal raisin cookies.

Manfred Eisenschmidtt was his name and you would have thought she had offered up a feast. *"Danke, danke, danke. Es ist gut. Sehr gut* (thanks, it's good, very good)," he said smiling and nodding enthusiastically. When they finished their coffee and cookies, Harold showed him his team of Belgians which Manfred greatly admired and then ran his hands in appreciation over their milk cows. *"Gut kuhen. Gut milch. Macht ost ya?"*

Anna could understand him a little better than the men so she said, "He likes our cows, thinks they are good milkers, and that we can make cheese."

As fast as Manfred came, he had to leave because the sun was getting lower in the western sky. He had no lantern and did not want to wander around the open grassland in the dark looking for his place. *"Auf wieder sehn. Danke kaffee und* cookie." After much smiling and waving, he was gone.

"Well, he seemed pleasant enough," Harold said.

"Yes, another lonely bachelor farmer out in the middle of nowhere," Anna observed.

They slept better that night under the quilts with the cheesecloth mosquito protection and were up early the next morning.

#

The next afternoon, a wagon came from the northwest driven by a blonde man with a young red-haired woman beside him. They didn't even get down before making introductions, "I'm being Kelly O'Neal and this be me lovely bride, Peggy." They were shaking hands as Harold helped them down.

"I'm Harold Kross. It's nice to hear someone speak English."

"We're no bloody English, we're good Irish through," Kelly said with a grin.

"This is my wife Anna and my cousin Oskar," Harold said. As the children gathered around, he added, "And these six imps are our children."

Peggy handed Anna a covered wicker basket filled with fresh baked bread. With a big hopeful smile, she said, "We are so happy to have another family so close. We were worried about another winter so far from any one."

Anna took the basket and gave Peggy a hug. "Thank you so much. This smells wonderful. It's going to be a while before I can bake anything out here." Taking Peggy by the hand, she led them over under the tarpaulin roof where their wood table and chairs had been unloaded. "Please forgive the mess, I haven't had a chance to sweep the dirt off my floor," she said with a wink and was rewarded with a laugh from the young couple. Without asking, she set her heavy white pottery mugs on the table and filled them with the ever-present coffee and fresh milk. It was graciously accepted. The children soon lost interest because there were no kids to play with. Johan and Anders kept working while the grownups talked.

"The neighbors we've met are not stiff-necked Dutch, but there's no even any Irish but at least none are them snobby English," Kelly said.

"We've only met one neighbor so far, a German fellow who can't speak English."

"Oh, yes, that Manfred, he's a hard worker that one. Seven days a week from the beginning of dawn to the last flicker of evening twilight." With a negative shake of his head, Kelly added, "He doesn't even rest on the Sabbath, but out here you have to be like Manfred or you won't get enough done before winter. We had luck with us because I had the cash for our twelve by sixteen wood shack with tarpaper on the outside to keep the weather out. An iron stove is your best friend in this winter that's coming."

Peggy cast an appreciative eye on Anna's cast iron stove sitting with its legs propped up level on some flat rocks. "What can you burn in any stove out here," Anna asked with worry in her voice. "There's hardly a tree in sight."

"You will have to spend some of your money at the railroad yard where they are bringing in piles of soft coal from west of here," Kelly said. "It's called lignite and it burns smoky and smells like sulfur. You need a real tight smoke stack though or you'll choke yourself out."

Peggy added, "At least it burns evenly and slowly so you can bake and cook with it, as long as you watch the damper on your stove's fire box."

Kelly eagerly added, "Manfred told me that he found a vein of coal in the hillside of the lake about five miles east of here." That had Harold and Anna's attention. "I'd be willing to go there with you, your boys, and Manfred and see how much coal we could dig ourselves." Harold gave an emphatic nod. Kelly continued, "We'd have to do it in the next month."

"Yes, of course, we'll come with. We have picks, crowbars, and shovels and our wagon is stout enough to carry coal." Harold was eager thinking about free coal.

"I was a coal miner back in Ireland. It was hard, dangerous, and dirty work and naught but a wage to starve on. I don't want to dig too deep around here because there's no timber to prop up a shaft."

"We'll not be missing that life in old Ireland," Peggy said soberly.

"Now, my dear wife, we must get back and get the chores done. These good people have more work than they can do in the daylight hours forthwith."

As the boys hitched their horses up and they climbed aboard, Kelly said, "There are some more homesteaders closer to town that you might have seen. Three Norwegian bachelors and one couple with a few kids and two Swedish and Danish families with about ten kids between them. North and east of us closer to the lake there are some Danes and more Norwegians. Mostly bachelors but a few women, too. There are two Icelander families northwest of here but the Norwegians and Swedes say they can't hardly understand a word they say."

Harold and Anna were glad to hear that there were more people than they thought but it was a broad landscape, especially with land so flat in every direction. "They seem to be good, stout, hardworking people," Kelly observed.

Peggy added, "Two city families came in last year but left in the middle of the winter on the train. It was too hard of a life for them was what they told the depot agent. If you want to know anything, ask Julian. He's honest and he hears the news on his telegraph."

#

In the following days, Harold used his big scythe to cut the tall grass around where the crates and wagon were sitting and started a haystack. He cut about four acres so at least the kids could run where Anna could see them and no wild beasts could sneak in unseen.

Manfred rode over the next afternoon again mostly to say hello. "Hello Anna, hello Harold," he called out with a big grin. "Have I for you prairie chickens!" He held up three fingers because he didn't know enough English to say more. "*Gut*, ahh gooooodt?" he said as he tried out some English words.

Anna reached up and took the big, plump prairie chickens he was holding out to her. "Manfred, these are wonderful. So big and fat. Thank you very much," she said as she gestured to her heart and then spread her hands wide to describe the chickens. In Norwegian she added her thanks, "*Tusen takk* (thousand thanks), Herr Manfred." She motioned for him to get down and come to the table for coffee. He enthusiastically jumped off the back of the workhorse. He didn't bother with a saddle and kept the horse collar on. The field he was working on was nearby.

He patted the big bay mare on the shoulder and said, "*Gut* Hilda. *Stille bitte* (quiet please)."

Anna caught part of that, "Your horse is called Hilda?" He nodded.

"Beautiful mare you have there, Manfred," Harold said as he looked her over more carefully while Manfred looked on proudly.

"Ya, have another horse and cows, too, Cora and Marta."

"Does the other horse have a name?"

"Ya, Schwartz!" They chuckled, then sat down to drink a cup of strong coffee.

"Is Schwartz a family name?" Oskar asked.

"No. Is color, Schwartz is . . ." Manfred pointed at the frying pan.

"His name is iron?" Oskar asked.

"No, he said 'color'." Harold chuckled. "He has a black horse named Schwartz which means black in German."

Manfred wasn't sure why they were laughing but after they sat down for coffee he said, "*Gut kaffee*. Strong." He made a muscle in his bicep jump. They laughed again. It was difficult to have a conversation but they were all bound and determined to try. Manfred asked in broken English if either had a sister who would marry him. Harold shrugged then shook his head no. Manfred looked very disappointed.

# # #

To change the awkward subject, Manfred blurted, "Haff you big gun? Shoots da wolves? *Viel* ahh . . . many wolf here." Harold shook his head no. "Wolf eat cow, horse, dog, baby," Manfred said very seriously. Harold still shook his head no. Manfred gulped the rest of his coffee and said, "Hour," pointing at his watch. Anna and Harold shrugged their shoulders having no idea what he was trying to tell them. Manfred jumped on Hilda and slapped her rump into a gallop, obviously not something he did very often as the mare startled forward. They disappeared into the tall grass within a hundred yards. They could hear the beat of the big horse's hooves on the prairie sod.

Harold and Anna looked at each other in dismay. "I think he's going home," Anna said. "He seemed to like the coffee, didn't he? Do you think he's upset with us?"

"Yes, he liked the coffee. Maybe he was mad because we said no sisters? He sure was in a hurry to go."

A half-hour later, Anders hollered, "Horse coming fast!"

Johan added, "I think its Manfred on Hilda again."

"What's the big rush? Is something wrong?" Anders scowled.

Hilda and Manfred burst through the tall grass straight to Harold and Anna. Stopping the horse suddenly, he jumped off with a huge smile on his face. "Here!" he cried, "Gun! Good gun," as he pulled something out of the work harness. He stepped forward to the puzzled family.

"Big gun! Bang, bang wolves," he said as he thrust a big infantry rifle into Harold's hands. Harold started to say no and refuse such a large gift but Manfred would not be denied. "Gun save babies! Wolves eat babies. Kill da wolves, you have to," he shouted.

"Harold, I think he means he's letting us have this big rifle to shoot any wolves that come around. He's saying they will eat the children if we don't kill them first." She looked at the big bore rifle in Harold's hands. "You tell him thank you! And ask him how to work such a big gun."

Harold looked from her to Manfred to the children and the cows standing nearby. He put out his right hand to Manfred, "Thank you, Manfred, my friend. Thank you so much."

As Manfred enthusiastically shook Harold's hand, he reached into his overalls pocket and pulled out a big handful of rifle cartridges. "Bullet, bang bang. Ya?" When everyone nodded, he was delighted. Manfred tied up his horse for the first time which puzzled Harold. Then he grabbed the leads from their horses and tied them to the wagon wheel. He pointed at the cows and ox that he wanted tied up, too. Mystified, Harold shrugged his shoulders and told the boys to tie up everything except the kids. He didn't know why but figured there was a reason for it.

Manfred came over and gently took the rifle from Harold. "Springfield, Army rifle," he said, holding up one of the cartridges so they could see the bottom where is said Springfield 45-70. Carefully, so everyone could see, he pulled the hammer back partway to the first click. He put his thumb under the little lever on the breach and lifted. The breach swung all the way up and he showed them that the rifle was not loaded.

Then he pulled an empty brass cartridge from his pocket and slid it into the breach until seated with only the base showing. He swung the hinged breach block down until the little lever on the side clicked. Turning so the rifle was pointed away from everybody, he pulled the hammer back all the way to the second click. Raising the rifle, he seated it extra tight against his shoulder and sighted down the barrel. He pulled the trigger and shouted "BANG" as the hammer clicked forward on the spent cartridge.

Anna and the children jumped. Manfred laughed, pulled the hammer back one click, and lifted the hinged breach block up flipping the empty cartridge into the air to fall on the ground. Manfred carefully picked up the empty cartridge and put it in his pocket. Then he pulled a live bullet from his pocket and showed it to each one, even the toddlers. Holding the rifle under his arm, he put a finger in each ear, then pointed at each and every one of them saying, "BANG."

Standing next to Harold, Manfred showed him how to put the live bullet in and click the block down. Then he pulled the hammer back to the live click and firmly set the rifle to his shoulder. He looked at everyone again.

Harold said loudly, "He's going to shoot and it's going to be loud. Put your fingers in your ears right now." When they all had done what he said, he did the same, and nodded at Manfred. Manfred gave a nod back and aimed at a small rock at the edge of the cut grass about fifty feet away. When he squeezed the trigger, the BANG was even louder than Harold had expected and the rock blew apart when the heavy metal-jacketed slug hit it square.

Everybody jumped this time. The boys whooped, but Anna had a frown and the littlest ones started to cry.

#

Harold smiled and Manfred smiled back. "Shoot wolf," Manfred said firmly. "Not eat babies," then he thrust the long rifle into Harold's hands and handed him a live round. Manfred watched closely as Harold clicked back the hammer and flipped up the breach ejecting the empty. Manfred said, "Ya, gooood."

Harold was an experienced hunter and had watched Manfred's demonstration carefully. He slid the live round into the chamber, closed the breach, clicked the hammer back off safe, and brought the rifle up to his shoulder. He was a good shot but had never fired such a large caliber rifle before. "Gray rock a foot right of the one he shot," he predicted. He aimed but hesitated while Manfred exaggeratedly plugged his ears so everybody else followed suit.

Harold fired and the gray rock exploded. His ears rang from the blast and his shoulder sure felt the kick. "This thing kicks like shooting both barrels of the shotgun at once," he exclaimed as he carefully clicked it on safe and ejected the empty.

He started to hand the rifle back to Manfred who shook his head no. "You rifle," Manfred said firmly, pointing to Harold. Then he handed Harold the handful of bullets and gave another handful to each boy and to Anna. He pointed at the rifle in Harold's hands and then at Anna. When Manfred said, "Anna shoot," she started to shake her head no.

Harold said, "Anna, you've fired the .22 and killed that skunk with one shot last summer. You've got to be able to shoot this rifle in case you need to sometime." Anna reluctantly nodded. He handed her the rifle and one bullet. She had been watching closely and went through the motions without hesitation.

"Black rock on the left," she said, then raised the rifle and aimed at the rock.

Manfred said, "*Stille*, Anna." She stopped. He bent down and pulled her right foot back and pushed the left foot forward for a better shooting stance.

"Manfred just saved you from getting knocked over when you shoot," Harold said. "Go ahead." Anna shuffled her feet pulling the butt of the rifle tight to her shoulder. Harold stood behind her in case she fell backwards. With mouth firmly closed, she sighted down the long heavy barrel and fired. The black rock leaped straight up in the air when the bullet hit the bottom of it.

As the kids cheered, she lowered the rifle with a little smile and shook her head. "I won't be able to hear the babies tonight."

Harold pointed to Oskar who did not hesitate to load, aim, and shoot dead center. Next Harold pointed at Anders. "You're twelve so this is going to be heavy for you. You've got to brace your front arm in front and hold it steady or you won't hit anything." Anders pulled a cartridge out of his pocket that Manfred had given him and went through the routine precisely. He had a little waver at the end of the barrel at first but set his feet like his mother had. He aimed and fired, rocked back half a step, missing his rock by a foot. He put the rifle down with a frown.

"That was a good first shot," his father said. "It kicks harder than the .22 doesn't it? Good job." He pointed at Johan who took the rifle eagerly. "Johan, you're almost as big as your brother so do the same thing." He followed the routine as good as the rest, carefully aimed, and fired. It staggered him back more than the others but he had the biggest smile because his rock had blown up. Hit square on. He gave Anders a playful punch to the shoulder. Harold took the rifle back, beaming with pride.

"Good job everyone," he said. "Boys, you did great. Now finish the job." The boys had frowns of confusion. Manfred pointed at the empty brass cartridges on the ground. They rushed to pick them up. "Be careful with those because we'll reload them."

Harold shook hands with Manfred in gratitude as did Anna, Oskar, and the boys in turn. Manfred had a smile from ear-to-ear. Harold tried to give him five dollars for the rifle but Manfred refused. He pointed to the coffee pot, "More *kaffee* ya?"

"Anytime my friend," Harold said as they and the boys sat down to celebrate.

Manfred pointed at his pocket watch. "Hours to work! Ya?" They all nodded.

Harold carefully hung the rifle from the tall head post of their bed. "No one touches this without asking mother or me unless there is a danger that needs to be handled immediately." Everyone nodded in agreement.

"Good folk! *Danke*," Manfred cried as he mounted the big horse and rode at a walk to his homestead through the grass.

"When we get some kind of a house I will make him a thank you cake."

Harold put his arm around her and gave an emphatic nod. "He'll want to marry you then so you'd better get a cousin of yours to come up here soon."

CHAPTER 5
Cutting and Burning

Harold cut more high grass to expand their yard and stacked the hay. They were warned that they would need lots of hay for the long, hard winter. This type of grass was not the best feed but the lusher grass in the coulee wasn't ready yet. Harold put together the steel moldboard plow and got the horse harnesses ready. They would have to cut sod for buildings soon but he needed to cut the grass short first.

A week after they arrived, still living in the tent, they heard and then saw a wicked thunderstorm rolling towards them. It was loud and there was lots of lightning but very few raindrops. One of the kids pointed to the horizon where they could see flickers of flame spreading. As the sun got a little higher, they watched the black smoke on the east and north horizons. It looked like the wind was driving it south, but as the sun rose, the wind switched more towards them.

Harold hollered, "Quick! Strike the tents. Throw everything that might burn into the wagon and the stone boat sledge." The urgency in his voice made everyone move fast. They started the ox and horses pulling the hurriedly loaded wagon and sledge toward the marshy ponds. They had to get away from the fire line.

"We can't outrun a prairie fire so get the cows and pigs into the coulee," Anna shouted. The smoke was getting closer fast. Tall sheets of fire were visible through the smoke in places. The animals were getting edgier as the smell of smoke got stronger and stung their eyes.

"You boys gonna stand there gawking until that fire roasts your hides?" Harold barked and waved for them to follow him. "Tie up some grass torches. We gotta backfire a line fifty yards or so west of the creek from this rock pile to that chokecherry bush down there." Harold, Oskar, Anders, and Johan each grabbed a shovel while Anna and the girls hauled buckets of water out of the slough ponds to dump on a line of dry grass short of the coulee. "That's where we'll stop our backfire," Harold yelled.

"Tuck your pants into your boots and button up your shirts and sleeves so the fire can't catch on you so easy," called Anna as she came carrying a bucket full of soaking wet bandanas. "Tie these over your nose and mouth to keep the smoke and fire out. Get rid of your straw hats too. They'll light up like matches." Harold, Oskar, and the boys ran up and down the line dragging their torches in the dry grass to get it going.

Lily and Kersta were only six and eight but they didn't hesitate when their mother told them to make sure all the men on the fire line had wet leather gloves before the fire got to them. "You can run through the smaller flames if you're fast enough,"

Harold advised, then added, "If you do catch on fire though, don't run or you'll burn faster. Roll on the ground to smother the flames. If you see anyone else whose clothes are burning, knock them down and roll them on the ground. God protect us all."

When their backfire had burned almost up to the wetted-down grass line, they smothered the smaller flames and embers with the flat backs of their steel shovels. They scurried up and down the line not allowing the backfire to flare up or send sparks ahead to the sanctuary where the wagons, animals, and all they had, including Anna and the other children were. It was desperate, hot work. The smoke was so thick in places they couldn't see a thing through stinging eyes streaming tears while the smoke made them cough despite the wet bandanas.

Anders wielded his shovel up and down the fire line while also stomping the smaller flickers of flames with his thick farm boots, on the run the whole time. Lily, with her dress tied tightly around her calves, ran back and forth with drinking water and dippers. A slurp of water was all they had to stop the coughing spells. She threw a dipperful of water in Anders' face. He pulled down his bandana and grinned. "Whew! I needed that."

"You dummy, your eyebrows and hair were smoking," Lily shouted.

"Stomp out the embers and move everything to the burned out area quick," Harold hollered.

Oskar was confused, "How the hell is that supposed to help?"

"Shut up and get moving! Listen up or we'll have animals burned and stampeded over the whole country." The younger children were not used to their father being so gruff. They didn't fully realize the seriousness of the situation.

Anna soaked brooms in the slough water and used them to slap out the sparks and embers being blown in on them. The sparks on the canvas covers were trying to flare in the wind, but her efforts shut them down. Anders and Johan used shovels to smother the grass embers. As long as everyone kept moving, the hot ground didn't burn their feet. Here and there they found little islands of cooler, packed down grass that had not burned. When the prairie fire blew up against the burnt east edge of the backfire line, it died out quicker than they could have imagined. Their streaming eyes and coughing eased as the breeze cleared it in the next hour.

#

The fast, wind-driven prairie fire roared around them, through the whole area. They were lucky they saw it coming and acted fast enough to save everything and everyone. Anna and Harold were grateful for the little creek that they'd been so disappointed in at first sight. They could easily have lost everything. He was relieved that his haystacks sitting in the coulee had survived.

Later they found out that some neighbors got burned out that day. Some were just unlucky while others had no idea how to fight it. Some backfired their grain and lost their first year's crop and some got some nasty burns. They heard two men later died from their burns. For Harold, it was a real loss because he had plans to cut and store lots more prairie grass for winter hay. When they came up the burned-over coulee banks and got to the top, they were astounded to see nothing but a black, crispy landscape to the horizons of the north, east, and south.

The next day Manfred came leading his precious horses. They could see they were limping. "*Wunderbar*, you all good, ya?" he called out as the family gathered around.

"Manfred, we were so worried about you. Are you hurt? Did you lose much?" Anna and Harold asked so fast that Manfred didn't have a chance to answer.

He shook his head. "Just haystack and small wagon." Pointing at his singed-off eyebrows he said, "Lose how you say?" Anna made him sit down so she could look to see where he was burned. "Gloves smoked, pants, boots, hot," he explained.

"Your hair needs to be trimmed because most of it is burned off like your eyebrows," Anna said. She pointed to her own eyebrows and had him say the word. "You have some burns on your cheeks and neck," she said pointing to them. She pulled out her can of Rawleigh's carbolic salve and gently dabbed some on every red area. "You sure are lucky not to have more burns than this. Does that feel better?"

Manfred smiled his appreciation, nodded, then said to Harold, "Hilda burn legs, Schwartz burn legs and belly. You look?" The big horses were obviously in distress. Much of the magnificent feathered hair on their legs had been burned off and there were blisters and oozing skin in places where the burns had gone deeper on the legs and the black gelding's belly. Harold shouted for Oskar to come and look.

#

Oskar ran over and examined Schwartz first who seemed to have gotten the worst of it. He then turned his attention to Hilda and was relieved to see that she wasn't as critical. "At least she's not burned anywhere except on the legs. I think their long leg hair must've started on fire. The gelding's in the worst shape. Anna, I'm probably going to be using up all your salve."

"That's why we brought it," she said firmly. "To use it when needed."

Oskar cut off the burned hair on both horses and used clean water to wash the dust out of the open wounds while the horses stood quivering. He started gently smearing a good coat of salve over the burns and blisters. They could see the horses' tight muscles relax as the ointment covered the raw flesh from the air. "They feel good now!" Manfred rejoiced.

Oskar asked Anna for clean cheesecloth to wrap the burns. "We gotta keep the flies off or they'll have maggots in no time," he explained. After they wrapped both horses' legs and the gelding's belly, he said, "Manfred, you must keep a close eye on their burns to see if they get any infection. We'll have to put more ointment and bandages on in a few days. Then we'll know more."

Manfred looked at them curiously. He did not understand everything Oskar said and asked if they could work. "No. Keep them quiet and make sure they have lots of water and feed." Oskar repeated it twice with many gestures and pointing.

Looking extremely worried, Manfred asked, "Leave horses here? You fix?"

"Yes, they can stay here. We'll do what we can," Anna said without hesitation.

Harold asked if he had any other horses. Manfred shook his head no. "Ox. Good strong worker." He held up two fingers and said, "Cows."

Harold said, "I'm going to hook up the wagon and give him a ride home. Wish we had extra horses to loan him but we have so much to do we can't give ours up for even a day." It was just the way it had to be.

#

Manfred's homestead was a long, low, sod house with a sod roof. It looked like one end was his barn. The fire had burned around it but since Manfred had plowed ground near his soddie, he hadn't lost too much.

"Straw stack burn. Wheat good. Big haystack good," Manfred said. Harold could see that one of the stacks had burned and there were the burnt remains of a light wagon still smoking some. He saw a big wagon sitting there safe. Two cows were eating from the haystack. There was a hand pump and a watering trough. The outhouse was not damaged.

"Garden good. Dig now," Manfred said. Harold figured he meant it was time to dig up the potatoes, rutabagas, and beets for the winter. He saw some yellow beans and onions, too. Manfred was apparently a good gardener and a good farmer. "*Danke*," Manfred said and shook Harold's hand. Harold wished he could stay and help but he had too much work of his own to get done.

As the Krosses walked over the burnt land they were startled to see so many rocks. "Looks like we could walk every acre of the place without putting a foot on the ground just by stepping from rock to rock," Harold mused.

Before turning a single plow furrow, they would have to spend many backbreaking hours picking rock. The rocks were left from glaciers about eight eons before. They were all sizes, some as big as a locomotive, and some the size of your fist. They couldn't move the enormous rocks so they would be the new boundaries for fields and pastures, and one even became part of a wall for their barn. At least no prairie wind could blow that down.

A pair of big rocks protruded up out of the ground. When they dug, they found they went down six feet. They dug the dirt out between them and put their tent roof over it for more shelter. Later they found some dead tree trunks in the coulee which they dragged up for a roof structure and sodded that over.

A soddie was cool in the summer and warm in the winter. It was crowded with nine people but better than living in a tent when the cold winds suddenly blew in before the middle of November. After they got a wood-framed house built, they planned to keep the soddie as a root cellar and storm shelter. Those rocks were good for something.

#

A nice rain started that night and lasted all the next day for a good ground soaking. The ash washed away and dissolved into the ground. It would act as a stimulus for new grass growth, an ancient cycle of nature on the Great Plains. Within days, fresh green grass sprouted up everywhere. Within a week, it was ankle high and every day it doubled in height.

The horses and cows ate well. It was the tender luscious grass that the prairie fire stimulated for the grazers to thrive on, just like the buffalo and deer had out there for thousands of years. They were the beneficiaries of prime fodder that would feed their stock until they could organize real hay and grain fields.

The burnt field areas and shorter grasses left the rocks visible enough to pick so they could start turning the sod with the steel moldboard plow. Thick sod slabs were turned root side up for hundreds of yards. The farmer in Harold gave him pride when he cut that first furrow straight and even from corner stone pile to corner stone pile. He had the boys cut the turned sod into two-foot-long pieces and load them onto the stone boat to pull to the new barn and house sites.

Twine was strung from stake to stake to form a rectangular outline for the barn. They started stacking sod up into rows two wide followed by another layer staggered. The third layer was laid crosswise and the pattern was repeated over and over. Within a few days, they had a barn of sod walls up to shoulder height with spaces left for doors and a couple of windows.

They had to cook with whatever they could find to burn. They were luckier than most because there were some branches and brush down by the sloughs they could gather. They burned wood in the cast iron range to cook their food and heat water for baths and laundry.

CHAPTER 6
Neighbors

The day after the fire, the Krosses were surprised to see three wagons pull into their farm led by the O'Neals. Peggy jumped down and hugged Anna, crying, "We were so afraid you'd all been burned up! Looks like you saved what you had."

The two other couples and their children came forward. "Harold, Anna, Oskar, this is Guro and Gustav Svenson. That's Art and Muriel Hansen. They're Swede and Dane." Without waiting for introductions, the three Svenson and four Hansen kids started playing with the Kross kids.

Each of the families had brought a small basket of food. Anna had Oskar help Anders put extra leaves in the table, then they all sat down while Anna poured coffee. There weren't enough chairs and the table was too small for nine grownups, so Harold and Oskar dragged over two smaller boxes and an end-gate board from the wagon to make a bench.

The other couples didn't speak much English yet but they all tried because that was the only language the Irish understood. Sometimes the Krosses had to use Norwegian to better communicate with the Svensons and the Hansens. They had some good conversations in spite of all the language differences.

The Svensons said they'd come over by steamship, then railroad right to their homestead last spring. They were surprised at what they found to say the least, but decided they could make a life out here. The Hansens had come to New York six years ago but decided they did not want to raise their kids in a dirty, dangerous, big city so they took their savings and filed for a homestead and bought most of what they needed out of the Sears catalog, including a small house. They moved in last fall.

Peggy's cheeks turned pink as she said, "We have something to tell you. We have a baby coming in the spring." Before she could even finish, the other three wives rushed to hug her and the men shook Kelly's hand and pounded him on the back. The women all said they would help when the time came. Everyone was all smiles.

"When are you due?" Anna asked.

"We think in March."

"Well," Anna said, "your baby will have a playmate then. Our next one is coming in March, too." They all clapped and raised their coffee cups in a toast.

#

Talk turned to the prairie fire as Harold asked the men if they lost much. "Some pasture and a few haystacks but only because we had been told to plow fire breaks around everything," Art said. "We had cut the tall grass to so it wasn't so dried out."

"We had harvested and shipped our wheat already," Gustav said, "so we're safe there. I put all of my oats in the sod barn so it was fine."

Muriel added, "It burned my clotheslines down so Art has to go to town and buy me a new one or his drawers won't dry." Everyone laughed except Art.

Harold said, "Maybe it burned up those grasshoppers we've been hearing about."

The men laughed, "If it did, we'd burn the plains every year. Probably won't help though."

"One good thing is we'll be able to see the grasshoppers coming because it's so flat here."

"Flat?" Muriel scoffed. "It's so flat here, I watched our dog run away for *three* days!" Everyone laughed.

Muriel said there was a new Danish Lutheran Church in town and everyone was invited. They didn't have a pastor yet but there were plenty of Bible readers anxious to preach the devil out of their souls.

"We had to make a rule that the service could only be two hours because we have so much work to do," Art said.

"He always gets a two-hour nap at church," his jolly wife added.

"We don't know which church to go to now that there's a new Catholic Church," Kelly said while trying to see how the others would react. "I was raised Catholic but was a poor one, and Peggy was raised Protestant. We got married by the captain on the ship after we ran away from home to be together."

"How romantic. It doesn't matter what you are. We're Lutherans," Anna said. "But we don't have time for anything else right now because we have to get our farm done before winter or we'll freeze."

"It looks like you have lots of sod to cut and lay up if you are going to get a house and barn done before the snow flies," Art said. "Snow might start in four to six weeks. Maybe before, maybe later, but rest assured, snow or not, the wind will come and freeze you to the bone. The weather is nothing to toy with, it can be deadly."

They soberly sipped their coffee, then Harold said, "We have lumber walls and roof panels that we brought on our flatcar. Oskar and I have to figure how to get them out here, but when we do, the house will go up fast. We need to make a bigger sod barn for our animals, can't risk them freezing to death on me."

Oskar added, "We would've moved the stuff here already but our wagon isn't big enough to load panels on and we don't want to ruin them by dragging them so far."

"We can help," Art said. "We'll fix our wagons together like a train and add our teams to pull it."

"By golly, that would work! Such a good and generous offer!"

"Kelly and I will help with our two wagons and horses, too. Maybe we can move it all in one day," Gustav said as Kelly nodded his agreement.

"A good old-fashioned house raising party it is!" Peggy clapped her hands with glee.

"It's going to be wet for a day or two but prairie wind dries things out quick," Art said. "How about we all meet here an hour after sunrise the day after tomorrow?" Everyone agreed and they all shook hands again as they left for home to get their own work done. As they were hitching their teams to their wagons, Art was looking around. "Nice cows, look like good milkers. Is the ox broken to the yoke yet?"

Harold nodded to both questions. "I've got a good strong matched team that I brought up from Minnesota."

"I thought I saw four draft horses when we came up," Gustav said.

"Those are Manfred's work horses. They got burned in the prairie fire so our horse expert here, Oskar, put ointment and bandages on to help," Anna explained.

"We'll know if either one of them is going to make it or not in a day or so. If the skin gets full of pus, they're likely done for," Oskar said grimly.

"Oh, that poor fellow. His animals are his best friends," Kelly said looking very concerned. It was clear that all of them had taken a liking to Manfred. "You make sure you invite Manfred to help move the panels or you'll be hurting his feelings."

#

Harold and the boys worked hard right up until an hour after sunrise two days later. They sent Anders over to Manfred's to invite him to help with the house if he had time. Anders came back saying, "Manfred wants to help but I doubt he understands what we are going to do." Shaking his head in amusement, he said, "He was busy plowing using a pair of cows yoked like oxen."

They picked the best squarish rocks they could find for a knee-high foundation of stone on the packed so they could add a raised wood floor later. It was hard work but they had a good, straight, and square foundation and a tightly fit stone platform for the iron kitchen stove.

When the three families with their big wagons and draft teams, and Manfred and his ox showed up exactly one hour after sunrise, Anna gave them all a quick cup of coffee and a couple of oatmeal raisin cookies to eat on their way to town. They took the wagon bed platforms off. Four wagons with six men and two boys left for town while the women got busy cooking, visiting, and gossiping while the children played.

This was the first time they actually had a day together to fan the flames of friendship. They had a lot in common being young, mothers or soon-to-be mothers, hardworking, and determined to succeed with their homestead adventures. They all liked to cook and bake and started exchanging recipes. They loved a good laugh, especially Muriel.

"Oh my, but there are so many handsome men around here," Peggy said. "Any plain single woman could come here and have her pick."

"Ya, I think you have something there. I have two widowed cousins in Denmark who are kind of plain. Not homely but not beautiful either. Good, hardworking women who despair on finding husbands. I'll write and suggest they come here or at least send their photos." They all laughed at such an outlandish idea.

"Surely glad I didn't have to send my picture to some old Irishman and beg for marriage," Peggy laughed. "I don't dare write my family to tell them where I am. I'll wait until I can send them a birth announcement and they can't do anything about it then."

Guro clapped her hands and laughed, then gave Peggy an unexpected hug. "You're a schemer for sure. I like you."

The women set about preparing a large dinner for noon or whenever the men showed up. They didn't know if it would take them an hour or all day to get back with the walls and roof. Anna's daughter Lily and eight-year-old, Sofia Svenson, were instant friends as they watched over the younger kids. They needed to keep them out from underfoot and away from bothering the mothers while they cooked and gossiped.

#

The men and horses were fresh and not used to pulling empty loads, so they made it to town in less than an hour despite the rough trails. Julian was glad that Harold was back to get the last of his things as they were taking up space in the busier than ever freight yard. They unwrapped the canvas covers from the panels and tipped them upright.

"We don't want to overload this trip," Harold said. "I'd rather take an extra trip than break something." They all agreed. They lifted and slid the first sixteen by eight-foot panel on one wagon frame and then a twelve by eight on top of it. They tied it tight so it wouldn't wiggle loose or tip over. They had moved the wagon axle pins for the double wagon to accommodate the load.

They looked it over closely before they hooked two teams to it. Manfred had left his oxen at Harold's place for the women in case they might need them. Oskar carefully drove the loaded wagon out of the yard and over the bump of the railroad tracks. It rocked a little but they just had to tighten a few of the guy- ropes.

Satisfied, they did the same with the next three panels on the other linked wagon wheel frames. It took less than half the time to get this one loaded and on the road. Art, Manfred, and Kelly drove one and Harold, Anders, and Johan drove the other. They kept the horses to a slow walk so they wouldn't break the walls and the windows installed back in Minnesota.

They were back at the homestead by eleven o'clock. Unloading went fast as they set up the wall panels on the stone foundations, nailing them firmly together. It looked impressive, sixteen by twenty-four feet and eight feet high. When they stopped for dinner, they were satisfied. Not one of the six windows or two doors were damaged.

Anders and Johan fed the horses oats and made sure they had enough water. They washed up and headed to where the women served up braised venison, potatoes, carrots, onions, rye bread, and coffee. "Don't eat too much now, we have to work hard this afternoon," Harold said with a wink. As soon as they finished eating, they hitched up and were back in town by two o'clock.

They had to adjust the axle pins because the roof panels were longer. They loaded three roof panels on each wagon and the rest of the lumber and rolls of tarpaper for the walls and roof.

Harold thanked Julian with a tin of Anna's oatmeal raisin cookies. It was a gift better than money because Julian's wife prohibited him from eating sweets. The cookies stayed at the depot in a locked drawer. Now and then when Harold or Anna had business or freight at the depot, Julian might quietly mention those delicious cookies. Cookie gifts became a tradition for them, never to be revealed to his pickle-faced wife.

They made even better time this trip because there were no windows to worry about. They quickly put up the curved top roof panels and got everything nailed down fast. They rolled out the tarred roll roofing, nailing it down as they went. The men looked at each other and nodded in satisfaction at how well they worked together. Language was not an impediment since gestures worked just fine.

They were going to carry the iron kitchen stove in until they realized the women had been cooking and baking in it all day and it was too hot. Harold said he and Oskar could do it later. Manfred said he would help, too.

Everyone pitched in to carry everything into the new homestead shack. They set up another plank table and benches in the house for all the kids for a noisy and fun early supper. As soon as they were done eating, the women washed the dishes and put stuff away while the men carried in the beds. They were very excited to have a roof over their heads and windows to keep the mosquitos out. The O'Neals, Svensons, Manfred, and the Hansens hurried home to milk cows and get some chores done before it got dark.

While the boys milked and did the chores, Oskar and Harold were busy putting tarpaper on the outside walls to keep the wind and cold out, then nailing up some wood shelves and plenty of nails to hang clothes on. They could not rest even after that. Fortunately, there were leftovers so cooking for the next few days was minimal. Anna let the fire go out after breakfast so the stove would cool down enough to be ready to move.

#

Sometime around mid-morning, Manfred came walking up. He was happy to see tarpaper on their brand-new house. He helped carry the cast iron stove into the house and set it on the flat stone platform.

"Manfred, I appreciate your help, but you have more work to do than two men so we don't want to keep you from that," Harold said.

Manfred's face fell. Oskar said quickly, "Let's look and see how your horses are doing. I've been watching but can't really tell much. I put more ointment and bandages on the second day. Didn't see any maggots and only a little pus. Let's hope it's no worse. Hilda's been eating and drinking which is a good sign but Schwartz is not doing as well."

The mare whickered softly when Manfred stroked her neck. "You miss me, ya," he crooned. Oskar carefully unwrapped her legs so they could stand back and look. "Not bad?" Manfred asked.

"We should be able to save Hilda but she will have lots of scar tissue that is going to make it mostly impossible for her to pull hard. She's better but Schwartz is getting worse. He's in misery," Oskar said solemnly as he and Manfred got down to look at the skin. "Some of this is open to the bone where the burn got too deep. Manfred, it is my opinion that Schwartz here should be put down. Now."

Manfred stood between his horses shaking his head with tears welling up in his eyes, "Is Hilda good for anything now or does she be shot also," he asked with a tremor in his voice.

Behind Manfred's back, Oskar shook his head no but Harold wouldn't have it. "Manfred, we can't save the gelding so if you want, we will put him down after you leave, but Hilda's a beautiful, big, strong horse just in her prime. You should keep her and use her as a brood mare. She'll throw lots of strong foals and Lord knows there's going to be a demand for draft horses up here. It will be worth your while."

Manfred looked from Harold to Oskar with hope in his eyes. "This is truth? She be good mama?"

"Damned right. You couldn't buy a better brood mare. I'm surprised you haven't done that already," Oskar said gruffly. Nodding but too emotional to speak, Manfred shook their hands, patted his gelding on neck, turned, and slowly walked Hilda home.

Oskar waited until Manfred and Hilda were over the rise. "Thought we'd have to shoot that mare, too. It would have completely broken his heart."

Harold went into the house and came out carrying the rifle. "I'll take him down to the other end of the property and put him out of his pain." Oskar nodded.

"Oskar you're a good horseman but why didn't you tell him that mare is already carrying a foal? Looks like she'll drop in the spring to me."

"I didn't even think to look past her legs. But now that you say it, I'm sure you're right." Oskar looked embarrassed having missed that. "I'll stop over to see them in a few days and take a closer look. If I can confirm the foal, I'll tell him. It'll make him happy."

"Yes, but it doesn't solve the problem of him not having a horse left to work anymore."

"He might be able to use her to ride to town if he doesn't push her too hard."

"I wonder if he has enough money to buy more workhorses," Oskar said as he silently wondered if the Johnson brothers would be interested in investing in some workhorses. It might be a good business up here.

CHAPTER 7
Coal Vein

There was no resting on their laurels. Early the next morning, Harold said, "We have to get the rest of the barn's sod walls up and dig and build an outhouse. Mother's tired of dumping the chamber pot. Oskar and I have to build the higher walls because the sod's too heavy for the rest of you to lift that high. More sod needs to be plowed, cut, and brought to us."

Oskar nodded, "I'll start stacking the walls and you do the plowing. We have enough sod cut to make it for a while."

Anna was more than busy with the three youngest kids, cooking, and helping with the horses when she could. "With all of you doing sod work, I'm going to have to take the wagon to town to get a couple more barrels of drinking water," she said.

Harold cautioned, "Be careful, and don't you go trying to lift anything heavy. I'll need one of the horses to plow with but one horse can handle a light load. Come back soon as you can, try not to spend what we don't have."

Oskar steadily stacked the sod higher in the same laying pattern. The first sods were short grass stubble which he started laying on top of the burnt sod. You could see a definite line from tan to black on the layers.

Anna and the kids returned in three hours with not only three barrels of fresh water but also four big sacks of lignite coal. "We need something to burn in the stove. This will last a few weeks maybe, then we'll need to dig our own or buy more from the railroad."

The following week, Oskar came across some Ukrainian homesteaders nearby who told him of free heating fuel laying on the land: dried piles of buffalo dung. In no time, Anna and the children were collecting wheelbarrows full of dried patties that they stacked in enormous piles against the outside walls of the house. Surprisingly, the patties burned hot, even, and odorless. They started collecting dry cow patties from then on, too.

The newest sod they cut was green so it added another color layer to the upper walls. The barn was not big, about twelve by twenty-five feet inside the two-foot thick sod walls, barely large enough to house the pigs, horses, cows, and ox. Chicken cages were hung from the walls. When they got sod up to over seven feet, they roofed it with the rest of their timbers and boards. They laid a sod roof on top with the grass side up, hammered together a barn door, and stuck in two small windows.

Oskar and Harold dug the outhouse hole eight-feet deep. A deep hole kept the flies out and the smell down. They had enough boards and planks for the two-holer seat and a door they could lock, to Anna's relief. "You don't know what you'll miss until you don't have it. Who'd have thought I would be so thankful for a simple outhouse I could lock."

Anna had the boys lay a wide rock path from the house door to the outhouse. Next they set big flat rocks for door stoops. Now that they had a cozy outhouse and a snug barn, they felt more prepared for the brutal winter they'd been warned about since they arrived. After the essential buildings and house were in place, they cut the coulee hay again and stacked it by the barn.

Anna wet and tamped down the dirt floor in the house. She made the boys bring in all the flat rocks they could find and laid them cobble style. It was still dirty, rough, and cold but at least they were not living on dirt like most still did. They dreamed of having real wood floors again. The Hansen's house ordered out of the Sears catalog was the envy of the wives but was considered an expensive luxury by the men.

In the next month, they had a hard freeze that covered the sloughs with ice. A few days later, Kelly rode over to talk to Harold. "Such a snug looking house and nice barn! The root cellar is a good idea, I'm going to build one, too."

"It's nice but the outhouse is pure luxury," Anna laughed.

"Could we all go talk to Manfred about going after that coal?" Kelly asked. There was no hesitation on Harold's part as he called for the older boys to hitch up the wagon. Anna heard Harold call for the wagon. She popped her head out the door of the barn asking if anything was wrong.

"No, not to worry. We want to see about the coal Manfred says is in the lakeshore."

"For heaven's sakes. Quit talking about it then and get out there," Anna said, standing with her hands on her hips. She shooed a cat away and tucked a loose strand of hair up into her headscarf. "My coal bags are getting empty and we haven't even tried to keep the shack warm except for cooking."

"Yes, Missus!" Kelly said with a laugh and a snappy salute. As the men finished the wagon hook up, Anna ran into the house and came out with a tin of cookies to take with. They loaded up and drove to Manfred's soddie. Manfred's dog started barking as they came in sight. Manfred came out waving.

"Hello!" he called, "Is trouble?"

"No, all's good," Oskar hollered back.

They tied up the team, and sat on the outside benches. Harold handed Manfred the cookie tin and said, "From Anna."

Manfred's face lit up as he lifted the lid for a peek. "*Mein Gott, Wunderbar*! Cookies." He smiled and offered them some but they politely declined.

Kelly said, "We'd like to find your coal in the lake bank over east of here."

"Ya sure! We go now, show where is!" He rushed into his soddie to put away his cookies and grab his rough work jacket. He brought out a stout pickax, a crowbar, and a heavy shovel.

As they loaded up, Harold said, "We better swing by home again to get some digging tools and tell Anna we'll be gone for a while, so she won't be worried. She still fears there might be Indians hiding down by the lake."

When they pulled into Harold's farm, they all laughed when they saw Anna standing in the yard with shovels, a pick, some sandwiches, and a water jug. "Here," she ordered. "Don't waste time. Take all these coal sacks. I hope there's enough to fill them." She loaded everything on the wagon before the men could get down. "I'll have cookies here when you get back, but only if you bring me coal!" She softened her words with a sweet smile. "Some wood would be nice, too, if there's any to be had." She put two single-bit axes on the wagon, then hollered "hee-yaw", slapping one of the draft horses on the rump.

With a wave, the men drove off east. Harold drove wherever Manfred said to. After an hour of bumping along the prairie trail, they came to the banks of a long, shallow lake. The banks were fifty feet high and steep. They drove south following the top edge of the bank. The lakeshore was still green in places with little ravines, streambeds full of bushes, and a few trees here and there.

Pointing at the trees, Kelly wrinkled his nose, "Cottonwoods. They stink like smelly socks when you burn them. Not good firewood anyway."

Manfred pointed to three big boulders on top of the bank. As they got closer, they saw they were covered with gold and gray-green lichen so they knew they were ancient. "We foot march here. Ya. Take tools!" They tied the horses to a chokecherry bush and followed Manfred down a winding path on the bank. The path was easy but wandered a long way north and then south as it went down. "Deer path," he explained. When they were most of the way down, Manfred led them off the trail into a little ravine. "Coal," he said, pointing to where a creek had washed out the bank.

Sure enough, they could see glistening black coal in the shadows. Kelly ran up and hit it with his pick with a clang. He picked up a piece and trotted it back to them. "Looks like coal," he said and sniffed, "Smells like coal." They handed the piece around. "If I knew what coal was supposed to taste like, I'd try that, too," he said with a huge grin.

"I hope you're right. Only one way to find out is to see if it burns," Harold declared. They gathered up dry grass, twigs, and brush branches. He raised his foot, and struck a blue-tipped match on the rough leather sole of his boot. It flared as he carefully lit the tinder and twigs. Oskar put some different sized coal pieces and coal dust in the edge of the fire. They watched closely hoping they'd hit the Mother Lode. In a few minutes, the coal started to burn with blue and orange flickering low flames. The coal smoke was yellowish and smelled like sulfur.

"Like I say, ya?" Manfred crowed. There were big grins all around the fire.

"Let's dig some coal," Kelly said enthusiastically. "I'll bring down the sacks."

Manfred, Oskar, and Harold didn't wait. They went to the vein and started digging out dirt and sod around the edges of the coal. Under a few inches of dirt, they hit more coal. Using crowbars, they probed out further trying to find the edge of the vein and how far up and down the slope the coal went. They each went about forty yards parallel to the bank but didn't reach an edge of the coal vein. As Manfred probed down the slope he finally found the coal edge ending in clay about six feet below. Harold probed further up the slope and clinked against coal as deep as he could probe.

Kelly rushed back with coal bags and food. He looked back and forth at the slope. "I think this vein is fifteen to eighteen feet thick and seems to keep running far to the north and south," he said. "It's very soft so it won't burn as hot, but at the same time we won't have to blast to break it up." Looking at both sides of the valley, he said, "Oskar, you have the youngest eyes. Tell me what you see straight across the lake about the same height above the lake as we are now."

Oskar and the others all squinted trying to see what Kelly might be talking about. Finally, Oskar said, "I think I see coal like this in those little ravines over there."

Kelly stood there silent in thought, looking back and forth and all around, and then gazed to the west where their homesteads were. "I might be dead wrong on this but I think we'd better see what our homestead papers say about mineral rights," He took a deep breath. "Did any of you hit coal when you dug your outhouses?" They shook their heads no. "I think there's a real possibility there might be a big vein of lignite coal under much of this area. It seems to me it might be this deep for a long ways, but I've dug veins that run and then stop or suddenly dive hundreds or thousands of feet. You never know for sure."

"Do you think we'll find enough coal to heat us for the winter?" Harold finally asked.

Kelly snorted and then smiled, "My good men, we might have enough coal here to heat us all for a century."

Pumping his fist, Manfred exclaimed, "Dig coal!"

#

They all jumped into the hard work, some breaking coal out of the vein with picks and crowbars while the others shoveled it into the bags. The coal vein layers broke up with fair ease. In less than an hour they had filled the burlap bags and pounded on them to get more in. By the time they were done, they had filled three of Kelly's bags, six for Harold, and two for Manfred.

They picked up their tools and each of them grabbed a bag of coal. Immediately it was obvious that wouldn't work as each bag must have weighed over two hundred pounds. It was going to take two men to carry each coal bag up the long slope to the wagon. "This will be a big wagon load if we can get it all up there. I wish we had some of those little coal cars on tracks now," Kelly said. "That's the last thing I ever thought I'd miss about Ireland."

"We can come back to get it tomorrow I suppose and pull it up on the sledge using my ox," Harold offered. "But then again, if we come back without coal, my good wife won't give us any cookies will she?"

Manfred smiled, "Carry coal, ya. This day, ya!"

As they carried their tools up the slope, Oskar said, "I think we have enough harness to use on each horse to make a packhorse rig and carry two bags per horse up the slope to the wagon. It might take a while but it's worth a try. If they can carry that much it would only be three trips."

The other men nodded and started figuring out how to make horse backpacks out of what they had with them. There were plenty of leather straps from the harness rigs but they didn't have boards to make the bottom of the slings. They led the horses down the easy path while they kept looking for wood. Looking as hard as they did, they only found chokecherry bushes. The cottonwoods they had seen earlier were on the other side of the lake. Oskar and Manfred went down the slope to the water's edge and after half an hour of searching they came back.

"We couldn't find wood but we found something that might work," Oskar said. "We need to take the horses down to get it."

"Of course," Harold said, "just be careful they don't fall or I'll make you carry the horse up the slope yourself."

"You two old men wait here," Oskar said to Harold and Kelly with a grin. "We'll be back quick." Before long they came back up the slope. Harold and Kelly burst out laughing as they got a closer look. Belted in with harness straps on each side at the bottom where the coal bags would sit were big white buffalo skulls with wide horns. The smooth sides of the skulls were faced into the horses' sides so they wouldn't be poked by the jagged underside.

"We found lots of these at the water's edge. Some were crumbly but these are solid as wood. We tried to break them on the rocks but couldn't," Oskar bragged and Manfred grinned. They loaded a coal bag on each side. It was odd-looking, but it worked. The horses weren't bothered and easily carried the heavy coal bags up in three trips. As soon as they were loaded, they headed for home with the four buffalo skulls sitting on top of the sacks like war trophies.

###

"My friends, I do not be knowing what the claiming laws of this United States have to say on mineral rights, but I be thinking we should look into the possibility of claiming the coal we have found. Do you know of this?" Kelly asked.

Harold thought for a while, "No, I have never known of any such mineral rights or claims. Might be my grandfather did but he's long passed."

"I've read stories of Americans going up to Alaska not that long ago and claiming sites for gold mining," Oskar said.

"It's something to check out quick before someone else claims it out from under us."

"I'm not one to trust shyster lawyers and I wouldn't know who to even talk to around here. Could be as soon as we mention it, somebody would take it all away from us. Let's not talk to anyone who doesn't already know about this coal yet," Harold said cautiously because he'd seen lawyers and the government take farms and land from people for less reason.

Manfred was trying to follow the conversation but there was too much said that he could not understand. "Keep secret, ya?" he asked.

"The only folks I know who have knowledge of this coal are us, our wives, the Hansens, and the Svensons," Kelly said. Harold nodded. As they pulled in to Harold's yard, Anna came running out to see.

"You have cookies please, Missus?" Manfred said with a big smile as he stood up in the wagon. "We have for you, coal!"

Anna clapped her hands in delight and laughed at the buffalo skulls, "Is there any more left out there?" All four men nodded enthusiastically.

"Hundred-year coal," Manfred announced.

"Oh my!" Anna exclaimed with her hand over her mouth. She looked at Harold questioning what was being said.

"Yes, he is probably right and there may be even more than that," Harold said with assuredness.

"Coffee? Ya?" Manfred was eager to get to the best part of the day, eating Anna's cookies and drinking her good coffee.

"Yes, yes of course. Come in, but not until you wash that coal dust off your hands and faces." She pointed to the wash basin by the kitchen door. Use soap, too!"

"Don't track dirt into Anna's house or you'll be in big trouble," Oskar grinned.

When they were cleaned up to Anna's standards, they sat at the table with coffee and fresh baked sour cream cookies. Anna said, "Well? Tell me everything!"

"We need to keep this our secret for now," Kelly said. "We are going to see if this might be something we could mineral claim like a gold mine before anybody else gets it."

"We don't know the law on claims but we'll find out. We think we should include the Svensons and the Hansens," Harold said. "We need to have a meeting with all of them to see what they think."

"We've got to get organized and mine as much coal for the winter as we can before the snow comes. The trail down to the lake will be impossible in the winter," Kelly said. Manfred was too busy gobbling down cookies and slurping his coffee to say anything, but he was listening and nodding his agreement.

"Today is Tuesday, so let's tell everyone to come here Friday unless it's raining," Anna said. "I will fix something to eat for noon dinner."

"Friday sounds good. I'll let the Hansens and Svensons know," Kelly said. "Let's do potluck. You haven't had time to plant food up here let alone harvest any."

"Vat potluck is?" Manfred looked puzzled.

"It's when everybody brings part of the dinner," Anna said.

"*Och*, ya, I see," Manfred said. "I bring deer."

"That would be nice Manfred," Oskar said, "but it's just for one meal and you must cook it before coming."

"Ya, I bring deer. Cooked." Manfred was emphatic. They finished their coffee while Manfred ate the last cookie and all the crumbs left on the dish with relish. He would have eaten a dozen more if they had been offered. "Crumb da best," Manfred said with a grin. They went out and moved three coal bags onto Kelly's trailer and stacked Harold's bags next to the kitchen door. Oskar drove the wagon to follow Kelly and help him unload his bags, then took Manfred and his coal home. After they unloaded the bags, they took a look at Hilda's legs.

When Oskar unwrapped the wounds, he sniffed each one. "No smell, that's good." He touched the healing scars carefully. "The blisters went down and I don't see any maggots." The mare flinched a few times, snorting when he touched sensitive spots on the wounds. "I don't like all this open area. I don't know if that much skin can grow back on some of it." He gently put on some more of the ointment. "Manfred, this is the last of our ointment. We don't have any more. Can you get any?"

Manfred shrugged, "Ya, maybe in town but no horse to ride."

"You can ride Hilda to town but only walk her both ways."

"Ya, is good?"

"Yes, but go slow and easy. It will be good to flex some of the scar tissue. Might help her mobility. Just keep the burns wrapped up and don't let her trot or run." After he was sure that Manfred understood what he was saying, he said goodbye and headed home.

CHAPTER 8
Spice, Coal, and School

Two mornings later, the neighbors arrived one at a time in their wagons. The wives came bearing heavy iron pots wrapped in quilts to keep them warm. Anna hustled the women and the potluck food into the shack and put the pots in the oven or on the stovetop. It was warm in there since they now had enough coal to heat the place. Oskar had set up a long trestle table with planks for the top and hammered together some crude benches for Anna.

Almost an hour later, Manfred came over the rise pushing a wheelbarrow with something wrapped in burlap bags. "Is deer," he announced. An enormous Dutch oven in the wheelbarrow was steaming. "Good fat doe. Ass?" he said, pointing at his hip.

"We call that a roast," Peggy giggled. Manfred and Oskar used heavy gloves to carry the Dutch oven inside onto the stovetop. The women were all curious and lifted the lid to look at the venison roast and take a sniff. "That smells wonderful, what did you put on it?"

"Mama cookbook say how," he smiled and held up a little German-English Dictionary. "English say, onion, thyme, rosemary, crushed black pepper, salt, cider. Just like Mama. Ya, good!" Who would have thought Manfred knew how to cook?

It was a real festive gathering. The Kellys brought cooked peas and carrots and Irish soda bread. The Svensons brought cooked rutabaga enough for an army and a big carrot cake with sour cream frosting. The Hansens brought pickled herring, sardines, and fresh oat bread. Anna and the girls had made pies from their stored apples and the big pumpkins whose time to use was coming to an end. They had made butter and buttermilk as well as rye bread.

Anna had spread flour sack towels on the plank table for a tablecloth. She only had one tablecloth and it was not even one-third the size of the table. Everybody found a place to sit. Peggy and Guro had brought extra plates and silverware because Anna didn't have enough.

"Manfred, slice your venison, and everyone else start dishing up," Anna said. Manfred sliced and sliced, loading up the largest platter. He heaped the onions into another bowl and poured the *au jus* into a crockery pitcher. Potatoes, mashed and buttered rutabaga, and the peas and carrots were passed round the table. It was even more delicious with new friends.

"All we need now is a Christmas tree to go with this feast," Gustav said in admiration. It was, indeed, a feast. They ate heartily, as hardworking farmers and growing kids needed lots of food to keep going. There was not much fat on any of them but after two (and in Manfred's case, three) plates full of everything, they were groaning in satisfaction. They were not bashful about wiping up the last drop of the venison *au jus* and every morsel from their plates with bread. They were so full that they agreed to wait for pie and coffee no matter how wonderful it smelled.

When the kids found out dessert would be served later, they went outside to play.

#

"We have some business to cover today," Kelly started. "Manfred led us to coal he found east of here. Harold, Manfred, Oskar, and I went over there a few days ago and sampled it."

"What did you find?" Gustav asked anxiously.

"You're feeling it right now," Anna said with a confident smile. "We're burning that very coal in my stove for cooking and heating our home." She picked a fist-sized lump out of the coal bucket and handed it to Gustav. He and Art nodded.

"The four of us mined twelve big bags in a few hours and are going back to get as much as we can. This is an enormous vein from what I could see," Kelly said.

"How big might that be? Enough for this winter?" Art asked anxiously.

"Oh, I'd say more than enough for a hundred years," Kelly said matter-of-factly.

The Hansens and the Svensons sat straight up in their chairs. "Oh my goodness," Muriel exclaimed. "Can that be?" Kelly, Harold, Manfred, and Oskar nodded simultaneously.

"We plan to share it with you if you want," Harold said. "It's just that we don't know what the laws are, so we don't know if we can make it a mining claim like the gold miners up in Alaska did in '97."

"We've been thinking that we should get all the coal we can right now without letting anybody else know about it," Kelly said. Art and Gustav were looking back and forth with great interest. They seemed ready to jump up and go dig coal immediately.

"Do any of you know about mineral claims? We don't know who to even ask. Might be soon as we ask they'll kick us off and take it away from us," Harold said very seriously. Gustav and Art said they didn't know anything about mineral claims but agreed that they should get what they could and be quick about it. They wouldn't say a word about it to anyone.

Discussion continued for another hour. It would save them all a lot of money not having to pay the railroad for coal. They agreed to meet the next morning with their heavy wagon boxes and tools. They would each bring an ox and a stone boat sledge to haul the coal up the slope. They would split the coal up with consideration given to family size.

"For example," Harold said, "Manfred doesn't need as much coal to heat his little soddie as the Hansens do with a bigger house and four kids." They all agreed that was fair and if it went well, they should go back as often as possible until the snow came.

#

Anna and the ladies made more coffee and served the pies and cakes. Muriel remarked on the cinnamon and pumpkin spice on the pies. "I used most of it up," Anna said. "I sure hope they have a traveling Rawleigh man out here like we had in Minnesota."

Peggy said, "There was a circular on the wall of the depot that a Rawleigh man is coming in on the train on November twentieth for two days at the depot. Maybe when this area gets settled more they will have someone traveling to the farms regularly."

"Oh, that's a relief," Anna and Guro said at the same time.

"You kids come in for pie now," Muriel hollered out the door. She had to step back to keep from getting trampled by yelling, sweaty, happy kids. They piled on the benches anxious for anything sweet. Once again, Manfred was a man of great appetite, eating two slices of each kind of pie and cake.

"Young man's got a hollow leg," Art laughed. Manfred smiled and nodded although it was doubtful he had any idea what that meant.

"No woman cook for me for year. This best in whole world."
He stood and bowed to each of the women, who giggled but were
very flattered.

"We'd better find Manfred a wife, one that can cook or at least
learn from him," Muriel said.

They divided leftovers so everyone went home with a little bit
of everything. Manfred insisted that they take all of the extra
twenty pounds or so of venison because he had so much more at
home. He was happy to have the other extras of food cooked by
"real women" loaded into his wheelbarrow. They hitched up their
wagons and gathered the children who howled their displeasure in
leaving when they were having so much fun. Everyone waved as
they headed home before the evening milking.

The next morning at sunrise they all showed up at Harold's.
The women and excited smaller kids stayed to help cook and play
while the men went to mine coal. The older boys drove the oxen.
Mining went fast and they had fun even for such dirty, back
breaking work. In four hours, they were back with heaping loads of
loose and bagged coal in every wagon box. The wheels and axles
were loaded to the maximum and groaning. Oxen each pulled a
sledge with more sacks of coal.

They went back for four days and the women used that time
for fall baking. They all worked until they were exhausted and

needed to get the rest of their own fall work completed. Everyone thought they had plenty of coal for the winter and maybe longer. Just seeing piles of coal close to their houses was very reassuring. Now they wouldn't have to worry about how much they burned for heat because it didn't cost anything except time and effort.

Harold, Oskar, and the boys finished nailing up the tarpaper with wood lathes. They noticed an immediate change in their house. Wind didn't whistle through the walls so the heat stayed in as long as the kids remembered to close the doors behind them. "Close the door, were you born in a barn?" was repeated at least twenty times a day. It was something kids never seemed to learn.

Everyone except toddlers had chores to do every day. Their homestead was shaping up into a good farm. They took a moment now and then to enjoy it. Beds were on the opposite wall furthest from the stove. Good use was made of the quilts and rugs they'd brought from Minnesota. Days were getting shorter and shorter, frosts turned into hard freezes, snow flurries turned into big snow storms. The howling wolves seemed closer.

Weather permitting, every few weeks they took a trip to the train depot to check for mail and buy necessary supplies. Manfred usually rode with them because Hilda couldn't be used for pulling and the snow seemed to bother her burns and scars. Oskar had told a delighted Manfred that Hilda was going to drop a foal in the spring and that Anna and Peggy O'Neal would have babies then, too.

###

The four wives and Manfred went by sleigh to the depot on the day the Rawleigh spice man was to be there. Manfred had insisted on going, saying, "I cook spice." There was no problem finding the salesman as a crowd of women packed around a little man in a brown suit and derby hat. He had a big sample case that he was trying to open. The women had rushed the depot platform as his train pulled in, tooting its whistle in a cloud of hissing steam.

Julian stepped out with two yardmen waving for Manfred to join them. He blew his agent's whistle and in a loud voice called out, "Ladies! Ladies! Please!" The crowd mostly quieted down. "This has to move someplace else. It's too dangerous on my arrival platform."

"Julian, there's not another train coming in for five hours," his wife hollered as she stepped out of the side door of the depot. "You let this man stay where you can keep him safe."

Turning red, he said, "Alright, alright! He can stay but we'll have some order here." He pointed to his yardmen and Manfred and the Rawleigh man saying, "You go to that end of the platform." Before the salesman could start, the women surged towards that end of the platform, too. "Hold it ladies! Get back where you were. Give him a chance to get set up and then everybody will get their turn."

He had the yardmen, with Manfred's help, gently herd the crowd of women away as the flustered salesman pulled his display case to the end of the rough platform. He set it up on end and unlatched the locks. It had four parts that hinged open displaying rack after rack, packed with spice tins. The ladies gasped and started moving forward again but the line of men held them back.

A large woman with a heavy Russian accent demanded, "Who first?"

Manfred spoke up, "All ladies in line. I count." Reluctantly, the fifty or sixty women formed a winding line. Manfred walked down the line pointing and counting off, "One, two, three, four, five, six", then again and again until he was at the end. He held up a die and rolled it to see which number came up first and so on.

Manfred explained. "First roll is three. All number threes raise hand." About a dozen hands went up including Guro's. "You first, fifteen minutes, then roll again."

There was some grumbling until the salesman announced, "Do it this way or I'll close my case and leave." The ladies who had the number three were let through the line of men and eagerly started their shopping. "Be reasonable. You can't buy it all, eighteen mixed cans each, no more. There's plenty enough to go around. Be patient," he announced in a kinder tone.

Anna, Peggy, and Muriel stayed together but they all had different numbers from the way they were lined up. Anna stepped up on a freight box and pulled the other two up with her. To their surprise, Anna shouted, "Ladies! Ladies! Can we have your attention? I don't know you but this must be almost all the women in Wesley County now. Let's take the opportunity to get to know each other. Introduce yourselves and shake hands."

Muriel repeated it in Danish and a woman in the crowd repeated it loudly in German. They got down and went around introducing themselves to as many women as they could. There seemed to be many languages but English and Norwegian seemed to be the most common. German, Swedish, Danish, Finnish, Russian, Ukrainian, and even French was what Anna thought she heard. She wrote down as many names as possible. Some were shy but most were anxious to meet new women friends.

Julian blew his whistle and hollered, "Fifteen minutes!" Manfred rolled the die and held up five fingers. Julian bellowed, "Fives, come forward!" The first group took their paid-for spices and stepped back into the crowd. They had heard the introduction idea and wanted to meet the others, too. It was a rare chance to chat and get to know other women.

In fifteen minutes, the whistle blew again and group number two had their chance, then four, one, and six. Anna was in the last group so Manfred joined them with a nod of approval by Julian and the salesman. They were able to get the spices they wanted but maybe not as much of each. Manfred bought a lot of exotic spices the ladies had bypassed.

"I want to thank you ladies and you, too, young fella," the salesman said with a nod to Manfred. "Here's a sample of some new cinnamon we're going to be introducing soon." He handed them each a fist-sized tin with the gold Rawleigh lettering and fancy scroll work. His display case was almost empty. "Alright! There's a little of this and that left. I don't want to lug it back to Minnesota so anybody who wants it can take two items for half price." Some women surged forward but most had spent their money already. In a few more minutes, his case was empty. "I'll be back December twentieth. Thank you kindly, ladies," he said with a tip of his hat.

Anna and the ladies looked curiously at the different spices Manfred had bought. No cinnamon, no pumpkin spice, no allspice. But he had thyme, rosemary, cardamom, garlic powder, basil, and the like. He even bought red pepper flakes, jalapeno flakes, dried ginger, tarragon, and curry. They must have been listed in his mother's cookbook. They were anxious to taste his cooking from now on.

#

Anna stepped up on the wood box again waving her hand for attention. "How many of you have children?" She raised her own hand and about two out of three women did the same. "How many of you are not married? Seven hands went up which got Manfred's attention. "Are any of you going to have babies soon?" Again, she raised her hand and so did more than a dozen. "Do you have a school anywhere?"

Julian stepped forward. "No, there is no school but we'd like to open one in town in the spring. We need to hire a teacher first."

"I'm not going to let my kids sit and do nothing all winter," a German-sounding lady said. "I'm going to teach my own kids and the neighbors' kids, too if they have a mind to."

That started a buzz. "I think that's a good idea," Anna shouted. "If you have close neighbors you should all try it. We don't want to be raising a bunch of dumbbells."

Manfred raised his hand, "Can I to school come, too?"

Anna looked at her neighbor ladies who just shrugged, so she said, "Don't see why not but it'll be in English not German."

"Ya, English. I know German."

# # #

The next week school started in the Kross house Tuesdays and Thursdays from ten a.m. to two o'clock p.m. It worked well as kids had to be home to help with chores in the morning and evening. With three families, there were fourteen children so the house was full. Peggy, Muriel, and Guro helped out as much as they could. Every student brought their lunch.

The women pooled their resources and set up lessons of reading, writing, arithmetic, and the like. They found slates, chalk, paper, and pencils that the kids shared. In spite of the age differences, class was held altogether. Older kids helped the younger ones. They assembled all the reading materials they had: books, newspapers, catalogs, Bibles, and even labels.

Poetry was read and memorized, spelling bees were held, and they practiced arithmetic tables and other basics of education. Sometimes one of the men would come in and tell a true story about something historic. Manfred was the star pupil because he studied all the time.

Harold and Anna invited their coal company friends for a potluck Thanksgiving since they had the biggest house. The kids had a ball. Adults broke out cards and a cribbage board. A few games of checkers and Chinese checkers added to the fun. It had snowed another foot the week before so the families came by sleigh or their wagons with runners replacing the wheels. It was lots of fun but everyone had to get home before dark to milk cows.

On the trip to town for more spices in December, they had mail and there was plenty of news and gossip. Newspapers new and old were brought home for more things to read for school.

CHAPTER 9
Winter Celebration

News spread quickly throughout the rural community of two more families who had pulled up stakes and abandoned their homesteads; 'taking the cure' they called it. Those that knew of them said they were from down south and couldn't take the cold and it wasn't even the deep cold of winter yet.

There was a very sobering story of a German family of eight found dead in their soddie that horrified even the bravest settlers. It was assumed that the stovepipe might have plugged up and they smothered. Everyone made sure to check their stovepipes after that. Farm animals in the soddie barn were attacked and killed, most likely by wolves. Even the dog had been killed. From the way it looked, wolves had dug through the roof. Life was not so sure out here on the northern plains.

One man whispered to Manfred, "Some say the wolves got the family too, but don't say that to the women or they'll all leave on the next train."

One school day, Muriel came with the bad news that wolves had killed their nineteen sheep and their sheep dog. Only the goat got away by climbing to the top of the outhouse roof.

Harold realized that Manfred was right to caution them about wolves. They started tracking and shooting them on sight. There were a lot more wolves then they had guessed. Coyotes were sneakier but they shot them, too. The Springfield 45-70 that Manfred gave them was good because they could hit their targets at five hundred yards when they got more experienced. Manfred had a second army rifle so it had not endangered him to give the extra one to the Krosses. He was a good friend.

Many of the Scandinavians had skis and were used to winter hunting. They collected plenty of bounties on wolf hides and also brought in plenty of venison and the odd elk and moose to eat. It made their food supplies stretch a lot further even without slaughtering oxen or pigs. Oskar soon became well known for his hunting and skiing skills. He could ski long distances in a day. He'd go out ten to fifteen miles some mornings and be home before dark, pulling a sled with his kills.

#

Manfred tried to meet the single women who had raised their hands in the Rawleigh crowd at the depot that day, but they either lived too far away or their families wouldn't let him court their young daughters. Two were widows and felt Manfred was not rich enough or mature enough for them anyhow. Too old for some, too young for others. He was very discouraged.

Anna had quietly written to two of her teenaged cousins in Minnesota touting the virtues of Manfred, but so far there were no takers. One girl sounded a little interested but she was barely seventeen and her father wouldn't allow it.

Oskar had hoped Manfred's mare's legs would have healed more by now. She was thickening up in the middle from the foal she was carrying. Oskar had asked what the stud looked like a few times until Manfred admitted he had no idea. He thought it must have happened the middle of last summer when he had gone to town to buy supplies and left her in the depot stockyard corral. He said with a laugh that he hoped it wasn't the Shetland pony.

The four families and Manfred planned Christmas together and had a wonderful time. They ate, sang, and played games. Some songs they could all sing together and some they could not, but they had fun. Christmas Day services were held in town even though there were no permanent ministers or priests there yet. They relied on circuit riders and when they were not available, some of the men of the congregation led the services. It did not hinder the celebration in the least.

Manfred, the O'Neals, Hansens, Svensons, and Krosses took turns visiting each other's homes to celebrate all twelve days of Christmas. Whenever they got together they all brought food to share and a fiddle or concertina to make more fun and music.

The weather cooperated and they didn't have to fight blizzards or extreme cold. They marveled at the clear, bright-blue sky, and the sun shining on the snow was so intense it hurt your eyes. Some evenings when the sky was clear with millions of stars shining and the moon was bright, they stayed together until far into the night because the men would go home to do chores and come back ready to celebrate some more. With the full moon, wolves howled louder and closer. Nobody went out without carrying a rifle. No one wanted to get eaten by wolves.

Holidays brought back thoughts of faraway family and friends. Even though they had made good friends on the prairie, they missed their families. The mail brought welcome and much read Christmas letters from back home.

The winter after Christmas seemed long, as Harold's father always said, "When days lengthen, winter strengthens." They had enough food and coal to cook and heat the house with, so it wasn't unbearable. Manfred always had extra provisions to share as he could only eat so much and he was a good hunter. He fished whenever he could and preferred ice fishing because winters were not so busy. They didn't have to eat any of their seed stock or butcher the ox who got even bigger and stronger eating the rougher hay that the horses didn't like much. The richer coulee grass hay was more to the horses' liking so they did not suffer from their winter diet.

Many Scandinavians were storytellers and often told stories that lasted for days. They learned that art by listening to the best storytellers in their families. It helped to pass the long winter. One such long, dark, cold winter day when the whole crew was visiting, Harold said, "Listen to those wolves. That darn howling stands the hair up on the back of my neck sometimes."

Seeing the look of fright on some of the children's faces, he said, "That reminds me of a tale my grandfather used to tell us." Anna, Oskar, and some of their kids had heard it many times but they still liked all the drama and sound effects. As they sat on the floor around their father, their eyes gleamed with anticipation. The others didn't know the story, so that made it even better. He spent a long time telling the tale to everyone's enjoyment except the little kids who got frightened.

Art told the classic "Three Billy Goats Gruff" which the kids always loved, and Kelly told the "Stone Soup" story to oohs and aahs.

Much of the joy of Christmas was being together and watching the children having so much fun. Each child got a small but special gift. Anders and Johan were given Sears jack knives with many blades. They were thrilled beyond words. Only men carried knives so that put a swagger into their step.

CHAPTER 10
New Babies

Manfred invited the four families to stop by his home during Christmas. His tiny soddie was decorated with lots of homemade items. He couldn't find a suitable Christmas tree and the ones at the railroad depot were ridiculously high priced, so he had a massive tumbleweed stuck in the snowbank outside with colorful decorations.

It was a nice winter day so they played games outside and took turns going in and having some chokecherry wine he had made last fall. Rich and powerful, it was an acquired taste to say the least. Oskar whispered in Anna's ear, "This would be better on flapjacks." She grinned and nodded.

Manfred's English had vastly improved since they first met him. Of course he was at their house many days a week to practice. He studied all the time and practiced words and phrases on everybody. The kids teased him but he just laughed with them and they learned some German, too. *Sheit*, and *scheiss* became unwelcome words as mothers found out their meanings.

#

One crispy morning in late January, Blondie started barking. Harold was in the barn and saw a sleigh he didn't recognize come in fast pulled by a team of matched horses. There were four fur-covered, fur-hatted men all waving so he went out to see who it might be.

In Norwegian he heard them say, "Hello! Harold, we are here for some of that good Norwegian wife cooking Anna told about last fall." Harold realized that under the mass of furs were the four Johnson brothers. They clambered out, shaking hands all around. Anna stuck her head out the door to see who it was.

"There she is, the beautiful Anna!" Lars called out. "Norwegian wife, cooking unmatched anywhere."

She laughed and waved, "You have a lot of faith don't you? Don't praise the cook until after you've tasted the food." Behind her she hollered, "Anders get your coat and boots and unhook these boys' horses and get them some water." In a minute, Anders was out the door unhitching the team and leading them to water.

"You have the easiest to find homestead by the coulee," Karl enthused.

"Come in, come in. Get those coats and boots off. Careful though, we have rock floors."

The brothers all laughed as Ivar said, "Bernt is so clumsy he might scuff it anyway."

"Harold, could your boys drag in that canvas bag from our sleigh for us," Lars asked.

"We got two wolves on the way over and they're on the back, too. Your boys can have them for the bounties," Bernt said. Johan pulled his boots and coat on as he ran out to tell Anders the good news. The two excited boys dragged in a big canvas bag.

"We didn't get here for Christmas but we found some wood and have been carving all the snowy days. Bernt is so clumsy he mostly cut his little finger off. But we sewed in back on. Bernt held up his hand and Anna was aghast to see dangling stitches in three different thread colors.

"Hold still," she said as she grabbed her sewing scissors and trimmed the ends tighter. "Why three colors?"

"Mama sent needles with thread with us from Norway and these were the only pieces left," Lars said. "Thread's expensive isn't it?" Anna just rolled her eyes.

Ivar teased, "Bernt cried like a baby when we sewed it up. Karl and I had to sit on him while Lars stitched it and now he won't let us pull the stitches out."

Anna looked closely at Bernt's finger. "It does look pretty well healed. I'll pull them out before you leave." She stifled a smile when Bernt grimaced.

The children gathered around when the brothers opened the bag. One at a time, the Johnsons reached in, pulling out hand-carved, painted wooden toys. They started with the littlest ones first and gave them all out including carvings for Oskar, Harold, and Anna. There were dolls, wagons, horses, boats, dogs, cats, spinning tops, a checkerboard, a cribbage board, and two wood bowls. The kids started playing with the toys right away but started fighting over them almost as quickly. The brothers laughed at that. "Just like back home in the old country."

"Boys, we have to go home and carve some more real quick," Lars said. "We missed one." The other brothers looked puzzled and alarmed that they'd left somebody out. Lars said, "Are you blind as bats? We need to carve a cradle before long." Anna blushed and Harold laughed when the other brothers looked startled. They were not used to being around women.

"We have over a month until the new baby arrives. Don't be worrying about it. But thank you," Anna told them. "Dinner will be ready in an hour if I can persuade you to stay."

"We wouldn't want to put you out any. But if you have enough we're kind of drooling," Karl said with a grin. Anna laughed and went to her range. She added a few things to the pots and winked at Harold. She pulled loaves of fresh white and rye bread and a cake out of the oven to cool a little before dinner. The brothers' noses were twitching appreciatively at the kitchen smells. They kept wandering over to see what was cooking in all the pots and pans, grinning all the time. She could hear their stomachs rumbling across the room.

Lily and Kersta set the table while Anna cut the bread and filled the big serving bowls. She made gravy while the big elk roast was resting before slicing it. "Please be seated," she invited.

The brothers were on their best behavior, minding their manners as if their grandmother was there watching. Bernt even stood to hold Anna's chair for her which earned him an extra smile.

Harold cut the roast as they passed the potatoes, rutabaga mash, cooked peas, and onion slices in vinegar. The brothers oohed and aahed at every dish. "Makes Bernt's oatmeal look pretty bleak doesn't it," Lars snickered. They all laughed including the kids even though they didn't understand what was so funny about oatmeal. While the ravenous brothers were getting second helpings and cleaning out every serving bowl, Lars said, "You have no idea how much we have missed potatoes. Could we get some seed potatoes from you for planting?" Halvor nodded.

Anna went to do some more at her kitchen bench. She had Lily clean the plates off the table and then serve more coffee while Anna brought out big slices of spice raisin and nut cake with brown sugar frosting. The brothers practically dropped their forks at that. They had to visibly hold back from attacking the dessert until Anna was seated. They savored every bite with little moans of pleasure.

"Next year you boys have to come for Christmas," Harold said which got a big smile from the four men.

"We'll come next year for sure," Lars replied.

They sat and talked about the gossip in town but not a word was said to them about the coal discovery, even though they were such nice young men. They said another family abandoned their homestead because half of them had pneumonia and needed to get to a hospital. The brothers didn't think they'd come back.

"They had a nice wood homestead house, too. Only about half the size of yours but nice and snug."

Oskar looked thoughtful and asked, "Where is it located?"

"About three miles south and a mile east of here," Lars said. Oskar nodded but didn't mention it again.

"Oskar if you're skiing down by us, make sure you stop for a bite and some coffee or if you are too far out to get home the same day we'll find a bunk for you. You might have to sleep with Bernt but he doesn't fart too much," Ivar said. Anna rolled her eyes as the men and kids laughed.

The brothers had to get home to milk before sundown which was before five o'clock. Anna grabbed Bernt by the arm and wouldn't let him put his coat on. When the others went out to hitch up the horses, she snipped and pulled the stitches out, and he didn't even whimper. She put some carbolic salve on the finger and wrapped it up. She patted him on the head like a little boy.

The brothers snuggled in under their horsehide blankets. Waving as they trotted out of sight, sleigh bells jingling so prettily to the *shusht, shusht, shusht* of the horses' hooves in the snow.

# # #

Harold and Anna made arrangements with the neighbors that if they saw a red blanket on top of their roof it meant Anna's time had come. With their snow-covered roof, it should be visible on a clear day. Even though this was Anna's eighth confinement, she wanted women to help her. Peggy was due to deliver her first baby in a few weeks, so if she could come, it might be helpful for her to see it all because she hadn't seen a baby born before.

There was always a possibility that no one would be able to get there if it was storming but Harold reassured her that he had delivered lots of calves and pigs and this wouldn't be much different. He was shocked when she pushed him with both hands on his chest and burst into tears. He thought that would be comforting to her but apparently not. Women were so puzzling. He decided he would fetch the neighbor women when her time came no matter if it was blowing a hundred miles an hour.

On the second Monday of March, Anna had Harold put up the red blanket and just to make sure the neighbor women would know it was Anna's time, they sent Oskar on skis to tell them also. Within two hours three sleighs arrived, dropping off the wives.

Harold hung blankets around the bed where Anna was lying. There were no separate rooms and it was too cold for the children to go outside, so this was the best he could do for privacy. Only the wives and occasionally Harold were allowed in the birthing area. Harold found lots of chores he had to do like chopping wood. He wasn't expected to hover over his wife. He couldn't bear to see her in such pain.

The kids, were mystified. Even the ten and twelve-year-olds hadn't noticed that their mother was going to have a baby and the adults never talked about it when children were around. The younger kids wanted to be with Mama but they had to settle for Oskar, Lily, or one of the neighbor ladies.

The older boys and Lily did their best to entertain and distract the three little ones. Lily had been in the room when her mother delivered Charles two years before and she was glad she didn't have to be in there this time. Even though she loved the babies when they arrived, she wasn't sure it was something she ever wanted to go through herself.

Nothing seemed to be happening behind the blankets for a long time. Women bustled in and out tending to Anna and making sure the kids were fed and doing alright. Guro told Anna that she had placed a sharp knife under the bed to cut the labor pains.

Anna thought it might be working until hard labor started. Muriel tied a sturdy rope to the footboard for Anna to pull on when she felt the urge to push. Peggy pretty much stayed in the background watching and wincing with every grimace Anna made. She wasn't sure this birthing process was such a wonderful thing, maybe ignorance was bliss.

Anna stifled her moans to spare the kids on the other side of the blankets and to preserve her modesty. Just at sunrise, a loud wail alerted everyone that a baby was born. Harold nearly ripped the blankets down rushing in to make sure his wife was alright. He was happy for the arrival of another healthy boy. She smiled tiredly at him, her face and hair sweaty. He thought she had never looked more beautiful and tenderly kissed her forehead. Then he rushed out so the others wouldn't see the tears in his eyes.

Peggy cried as she held the newborn. She could hardly wait until her own baby was born but was worried if she could endure it all. Muriel and Guro stood by smiling proudly that they had helped deliver the first baby born in their township. The little kids didn't like the new baby crying so they started to cry, too. The women cleaned up Anna and the baby so the children could come in to meet their new brother William. Anna would remain in bed for almost a week as was common in those days.

Later on that day, Oskar drove Guro and Muriel home in the sleigh to tend to their own children. Peggy stayed to help for two more days, then Guro and Muriel took turns coming over for a few hours every day. It was good for Peggy to have time to talk with Anna more about giving birth. Peggy had never seen a birth before so this was eye-opening and alarming. Anna tried to reassure her, "If it was so terrible do you think any of us would have had more than one?" Anna didn't tell her that the first one can be real long, hard, and painful beyond belief. There was no use in scaring her, after all, she'd find out for herself all too soon.

The baby woke up crying every two hours to be fed and changed. In the small homestead shack there was no place to get away from the noise except to go out to the barn to milk and do the chores. The older kids took turns staying in with the younger ones who needed to be entertained to keep them from climbing on the bed with Mama like they wanted to. She needed her rest.

#

A month later, Peggy went into labor. The wives were summoned by a panicky Kelly at the first hint of labor, but they all understood. Anna was feeling strong enough for Harold to take her and the baby over there bundled up in the sleigh. All three wives were there and it was a good thing, because they were all desperately needed during Peggy's three-day labor that wore her out almost to death. Kelly was terrified that he was going to lose both his wife and baby and he refused to leave her side.

Peggy was so exhausted she couldn't push any more but the self-appointed midwives told her she had to do it, the baby had to come out as soon as possible. They shared worried looks with each other, all afraid the baby or mother or, God forbid, both would be lost. When the baby finally slid out into Guro's strong hands, it made no sound.

Kelly was as white as a sheet. Without hesitation, Guro put her finger in the baby's mouth to clear the mucus, turned the baby over and smacked her back. Finally, a mewling cry was heard and everyone burst into happy tears.

Mary Catherine O'Neal was tiny but healthy. Muriel put her to her mother's breast where she eagerly latched on and started nursing. Kelly was wide-eyed with amazement. "Look at her!" he cried, tears rolling unabashedly down his face. He kissed and kissed his wife's face until the other women gently moved him aside so they could tend to Peggy and the other events that followed childbirth.

They sat Kelly down on a rocking chair and handed him his cleaned up, tightly-bundled daughter. He barely moved as he held her, maybe not even breathing for a time as he fell completely in love with this tiny little person they had created.

Peggy was completely exhausted having lost a lot of blood. She was very weak but she came around by the time spring arrived. She and Kelly were in love more than ever and doted on their tiny baby girl. The other wives remembered back to those magical first days of parenthood. They had no intention of telling them it was not going to be all smiles and kisses!

# # #

With the drama of the births and the long winter, everyone was anxious for the spring thaw so they could finish breaking up sod and get their sowing done. Anna, Harold, Oskar, and Manfred carefully planned their garden plantings by the moon phases like they had always done with the Farmer's Almanac.

Spring came later than they were used to but when it hit, everything thawed fast. They heard the water start to run before the ice melted and within days the marshy creek bed was a fifty-foot-wide river of rushing, foaming water. They worried it would keep spreading to their barn and shack but were relieved when it stayed pretty well to the edges of the coulee. "This must be the river you saw on the homestead land map," Anna said.

It ran fast and wide for a week, then slowed down until it was ten feet wide through the middle of summer when it dried back down to the marsh and ponds they had found last fall. Ducks, geese, and cranes came back as soon as the snow melted. They hunted enough to eat but didn't slaughter big numbers like they could have. There were swans that came in to feed during the day but flew back to the lake at sundown.

"Only the snobbish royals had swans back in Britain and Scandinavia," Kelly said. "We're not royals but the swans don't know that and we're not going to tell them!" They all laughed.

He wasn't a snob but had a taste for better, more modern things, and tried to get them as soon as he could afford it. They bought a good wood house from Sears and not much later bought a Dutch-roofed barn. "Back in Ireland we had electric street cars, gas lights in the houses, telephones, and electric lights in the shops. There was even a motion picture show and music on Mister Edison's gramophone in the mining town where we lived. Most of us coalminers could barely afford food for our families so those luxuries were only there to tease us."

"We had some of those things in our town and the bigger towns like Woburn but never a moving picture show. That must be something," Anna said.

"There were troubles coming in our mining town and lots more across Ireland," Kelly said with troubled eyes. "Agitators were saying we should strike and burn the English snobs' houses and fight the bloody Redcoats."

"Yes, and what would I have been left with if you did that?" Peggy said with a grimace. "Widow's weeds, a burned-down village, and soldiers with guns driving us out like sheep."

"It's going to happen sooner or later. We're thankful to be gone before it happens."

"My uncles fought in the Civil War and from what they said, it was hell and death all together," Harold shook his head. "Us Americans know enough now to never get into another shooting war."

As the snow melted and the ground thawed, they started breaking more sod. The fire had made it easier because they could see the rocks before they broke plow laces on them. The sod was tough and deep. Harold's Belgian team wore themselves out every day. They were worn out every morning after three hours and had to rest until midafternoon when they could break sod for another couple of hours. Even though he was using a steel moldboard plow, it was tough going to turn over two acres a day.

Harold had to get as many acres broken and sown as fast as he could. Just turning the sod was not enough to make the ground ready for seed. He had Oskar use the ox to run the disc harrow over the turned sod time after time but it was still not the soft soil that he wanted for sowing.

#

When Manfred came visiting, anxious for some of Anna's cookies, he shook his head at Harold's farming efforts. "You need to do more work on the ground. It took me a whole summer before I could plant my wheat."

In exasperation, Harold said gruffly, "The Johnson boys said they planted many acres the first year!"

"Ya, ya they did!" Manfred said, hands in the air, palms out to placate his friend. "But there were four of them and they have three draft horse teams and four oxen! Those boys work sixteen hours a day and never take a day off. They killed one team from overwork. You don't want to do that."

"I can't afford another team and I need to get some wheat in to sell," Harold huffed.

"I think with your team and ox you can get fifteen to twenty acres ready and planted this year. You have three or four weeks to get the ground ready and seeded but your harvest will be late and that's always a danger here because snow or frost might get it before you can harvest it. You need to put in some oats and rye, too. They can go in later than wheat because they ripen quicker. Besides that, you need oats for your stock and rye for your bread. Wheat is too valuable to eat when you can sell it for cash. That's what I do it and so do the Johnsons and most others."

Harold wasn't quite so upset now and he and Oskar were nodding in agreement. They understood that Manfred had been here longer and was just trying to help them. "If you get ten or twelve acres of oats and rye in, that should feed your farm for a year if the grasshoppers don't eat it up first," Manfred said. "That happens to every field in places. Damned grasshoppers! I would help you but with my only horse lame I only have the ox and cows to pull the harrow. I will be lucky to plant twenty acres like last year even though my ground is mostly ready."

"Manfred, you have helped us more than we can ever thank you for. We would like to help you but we need to get as much of ours done as possible. We have a big family to feed."

"Ya, take care of your own first. Maybe more horses will come in that I could buy, but I don't have money for that until the wheat is harvested."

Harold nodded, "You've given me an idea. Maybe we can train our big cows to pull a harrow, too." So that's what they did. Oskar trained and drove the cow team, Anders drove the ox, and Harold drove the horses and plow. It definitely helped get more acres planted.

#

A few weeks later, Oskar drove to town to see if there was any mail and to buy salt and flour. After supper, he pulled a letter out of his pocket and handed it to Harold. "From my father and Uncle John," he said. "I wrote them about my idea to fix our horse problem. They will help me do this to get into the horse business."

Harold was curious, "What horse business would that be and how?"

"You'd have to help me convince Manfred to give up Hilda."

"He loves that mare like a wife. He won't give her up."

"He might if you can convince him that she would do better by sending her down to my uncle's farm to breed with his big Belgian stud and be a brood mare. She could be a cart horse down there because the climate is not as harsh. Besides that, my father is a better horse healer than me and he can get her healthier. She likely won't last another year here, the cold is too painful for her burns."

"So Manfred would be trading Hilda and the foal she's carrying for what?"

"Father will send Manfred an older team of Percherons and us a young team of Belgians for the summer work."

Harold's eyebrows went up in surprise. "We best go see Manfred in the morning and see what he says."

"No, send Lily over and invite him for supper tomorrow. He'll listen better because he likes my cooking," Anna said.

"You always were the smart one, Anna," Oskar said as Harold nodded.

The next morning Lily, escorted by Blondie, walked to Manfred's. Lily was too small to handle the heavy work of plowing sod or harrowing so she was glad to get out of breaking up sod with a shovel for a garden. She whistled all the way. Manfred was delighted with the invitation. That night he arrived on his mare. "Can't have her pull yet, but she's okay with this," he said.

Supper was wonderful. Manfred was all smiles, amenable to second and third helpings of most everything. When they were done with apple pie and coffee, Harold and Oskar explained their proposal and the likelihood of Hilda living a better, longer life if she was sent to Oskar's father's farm for breeding.

Manfred listened carefully because he still did not understand a lot of what was said the first time. "My Hilda go in boxcar to Minnesota?" Harold and Oskar nodded. "Have foal there? Breed with big strong stud every year? Live long life and not suffer from cold on scars?" Oskar and Harold nodded after each question.

"My father knows how to heal horses and would keep her legs in socks in the cold and not take her out of the barn in the snow. She could live ten years there instead of one here."

"I get two big Percherons now if I send Hilda?"

"Yes, and Oskar's uncle will send us a pair of Belgians to work up here in the summer but they might go back to Minnesota to foal. Oskar wants to be a horse breeder and dealer."

Oskar nodded enthusiastically, "Everybody up here needs more good, affordable horses, us included."

Manfred stood up, extending his hand to Oskar and then to Harold. "We have business! Ya!" Pausing, he ordered, "Send Hilda on train this week. Fast."

Oskar was way ahead of him, "There is a freight with stock cars for shipping that I can go on with Hilda in three days and I can be back in a week with the four draft horses.

When Manfred and Oskar took Hilda to the train depot, Manfred had tears in his eyes. Hilda had been his friend and workmate for two years on the lonely prairie. He knew it was best for her though. "*Auf wiedersehen mein liebschen,*" he whispered in her ear. Then he quickly turned to walk home, not looking back or waiting for the train to take her away.

CHAPTER 11
A New Bride

As promised, Oskar arrived back from Tranquil on the train a week later with two fine teams of horses as well as a box of older puppies and another of big kittens that their old neighbors were anxious to get rid of. Manfred claimed two female pups and a kitten on the spot. "Next time bring girl cousins you talk about," he said.

Oskar's father and uncle had sent along some old but good harnesses and horse collar rigs that fit the big teams. Within hours, they drove the teams to the two homesteads and in no time at all, they were at work. The horses thrived on the hard work with clean water, oats, and lots of fresh green grass. The prairie fire had cleared out the tough-stalked grass and allowed luxurious growth of new, tender grass. It grew as fast as they could scythe it down for hay.

That summer they hayed much of it three times, with enough hay for winter and even some to sell. They plowed and disc harrowed more than they had hoped to.

Manfred loved his seasoned strong team of mares, and true to form, he treated them like family and immediately dubbed them Gretel and Gretchen. Harold and Oskar each drove their teams from sunup to sundown every day. Johan and Anders drove the ox and cow team disc harrowing and hauling rocks out of the fields. Anna and the girls were busy day and night cooking, baking, and working the ground for a big garden. It was hard work and everyone had to help. There were no arguments at bedtime, they just fell into bed and slept like stone trolls.

When it rained, they fixed harness and did more building in the shack and barn. They bought barbed wire and fence posts to enclose the pasture and corral to keep the animals in. Both cows had dropped healthy calves that spring, two little heifers, so they would have them for milk cows in a few years. Increasing the herd was what it was all about.

Seed had to be hand-broadcasted for wheat, oats, and rye. It was a lot of area to cover, followed up by the younger boys with a toothed drag to lightly bury the seeds so they would germinate in the moist ground and keep the birds from eating it all. Blondie kept busy running around barking and chasing the birds off while they seeded. They set up scarecrows which helped, too. When a big flock of red-winged blackbirds descended on a freshly seeded field, a pair of red-tailed hawks came in and hit some of them which scared the flock away.

"Never shoot at a hawk unless he's after your chickens," Harold said, "and don't disturb their nests either." Hawks had been following the plowing, swooping out of the sky to snatch up gophers and mice as their burrows were disturbed. It was fun to watch them.

Oskar said, "The same goes for red-winged blackbird nests in the marsh. But why are there so many white seagulls out here? There's no ocean for fifteen hundred miles."

Harold shrugged, "I don't know but they can stay as long as they eat a lot of grasshoppers."

Bit by bit they were improving their farm and doing the never-ending chores. Anna had the small boys and girls digging, planting, and weeding the garden. From the start, they discovered how much wild critters loved tender garden plants. Gophers, raccoons, and field mice ate some of the plants as fast as they came up. Even the chicken wire fence couldn't keep them out. Keeping the cats hungry so they hunted the garden at night was the best way to control it. Art had given them a pair of cats and by the middle of summer there were two batches of kittens. Even extra cats were in demand by the new neighbors. Blondie whelped seven puppies in June and the neighbors were offering trade for them. By the end of July all the puppies had been adopted.

#

From the very start, the Kross farm was successful. Virgin prairie sod was pretty flat and not bound up by trees or brush, making it easier to break into big fields, only having to deal with a never-ending supply of rocks.

The kids discovered by taking a shovelful of red ants and dropping it on a black ant pile, the ants would go to war with each other. Oh, how they would fight. Entertainment was sorely lacking so kids made do with what they found. They snared gophers and collected the tails that the state paid a penny bounty for.

They encountered some vicious badgers that had to be shot or they would kill calves, dogs, and cats. They were afraid of nothing and would attack you if you didn't kill them first.

They learned about grasshoppers that took about a fourth of their wheat, rye, and oats before ripening late that year. They cut their own grain, bundled, and stacked it up in shocks in the fields to dry until they were gathered. A threshing crew with a big threshing machine and steam engine set up on the farm where they and their neighbors worked together. Within a week, their sheaves were run through the threshing machine and the grain sacked in bushel bags. They worked together until everyone's grain was harvested, then the threshing crew and machines moved on.

It was expensive but they knew there was no other way. The women had spent a week cooking and getting ready to feed the crews. It was a time of joy, the reaping and selling time when they found they had enough money to keep going and maybe even enough to buy some fantasy store goods and farm equipment. The price of wheat went up for a few years but then slowly went down, a trend that continued through several decades.

There were too many neighbor kids to school in Harold's home that winter so neighbors got together and built a new one-room schoolhouse with a coal-burning stove, slate blackboard, wood benches, and desks. They had a three-part outhouse for the children and a single for the teacher. The first year the farm wives had taken turns teaching the kids but now there were over thirty kids in grades one through eight and it was just too much for them with their own farms and households to run.

A young woman from Minnesota answered the ad for a schoolteacher. She had attended a whole year of Normal School (Teachers College) and spoke Norwegian, Swedish, and German as well as English. This would be a great advantage because most of the kids at home still talked the language of their immigrant parents. Miss Sorenson was nineteen and eager to teach.

A female teacher was not allowed to be married because married women usually became pregnant and what if the kids asked about such a thing? Never mind that many families had a dozen kids, most all born at home with the children around.

They worked out that the teacher would spend a few weeks living and eating with each of the families of kids in school. Most of it worked out but not every place was ideal. Some gave her a bed, great food, and a ride to and from school each day. Others did not have as much food or were stingy with it. Sometimes there would be young males in the house who would be too romantically inclined towards her. She had signed a standard teacher contract saying she would teach for a year without getting married and could be signed up each year if she kept that promise.

She had to be a firm disciplinarian for kids who ranged from in age from five to fifteen as well as many adults who wanted to continue their education. She taught a lot of evening classes, many of them for English. Her language skills were greatly appreciated and more than a few bachelor farmers fell in love with her. That made for difficulty sometimes and the older husbands would then have to have a serious talk with the suitor to dissuade his amorous endeavors. After all, a good teacher was to be protected, whether she wanted to be or not.

Manfred and Oskar were two of those who attended every class they could find time for. Manfred was shy enough that he was not one of the pesky ones. Oskar appreciated Miss Sorenson but he was having a romance by mail with a girl from back home. Manfred said he had tried to have a romance by mail with girls back home in Germany but with letters taking almost a month to get delivered, it was hard to build up much ardor on anyone's part. He also might have been too honest in describing how hard his life on the prairie was.

# # #

The next few years went fast with plenty of work as the kids got bigger and took on more and more chores as they were able.

Johan and Anders got bigger and stronger so they did men's work as was expected of them. With four of them and another added team of draft horses they broke more land for growing wheat and barley to sell and oats for animal feed and rye for the family bread. The price of wheat jumped again for a few years so they were able to buy better equipment and more horses. It was a prosperous time.

Trains bearing more settlers kept arriving. Soon most of the sections were homesteaded and settled. Some came to make a new farm home community and some were there just to claim the land long enough to sell it. Not everyone was successful. Some didn't have the skills or work ethic to succeed. Others started with loan debt and could never get out while some tried to farm the wrong crops on the wrong kind of soil in the wrong climate.

More than a few just gave up or were too lonely to stick it out. Some couldn't take living in primitive conditions for any length of time. Sickness and depression were enough to destroy some folks. Some were so intolerant that they couldn't live near anyone different from them be it race, religion, or ethnicity. The Irish were suspicious of the English and the Norwegians had animosity towards the Swedes. But for the most part, they were young, family-oriented, ready to succeed, and willing to work at building a community with schools and churches.

The Scandinavians gathered together and built a Lutheran Church but in a short time they escalated the argument about if services would be in Norwegian or Swedish or Danish. Since there were few Danes, they sided with the Norwegians. They could not reach any agreement except to take big buck saws and cut the church in two and put the front half with the altar on one site and the entry half on another site. Then they each filled in the missing part when they had the time and money to build it. After another twenty years, the problem solved itself because all the services at both churches were in English.

#

Over the next years they worked hard, breaking more sod, building more fences, breeding more stock, and building more structures needed on the farm. The railroad depot thrived. There was a fast influx of merchants' stores, liveries, banks, churches, a school, and a high school after a few years. They even built a doctor's office with a few beds. Of course, there were saloons and a dance hall. The railroad built a hotel and a café.

Lots of houses sprang up, some elegant, many humble, and a few hovels. The town constructed board sidewalks on Main Street which varied between mud, dust, and frozen ruts. By far the easiest way to get around was when they were covered with snow and ice. The roads in the county were the same way. It was much easier to pull heavy loads over the snow than rails and what passed for roads for decades to come.

A steady stream of homesteaders left for a multitude of reasons so there was land to buy up at reasonable prices. Most still distrusted banks and only bought with cash.

Oskar was having good success with workhorse trading and breeding. His father and uncle were his partners helping to buy and breed horses in southern Minnesota where more horses were available. He was doing well enough that when a bachelor farmer on a quarter section pretty close to Harold's with a wood barn and a small homestead shack decided to go further west to Oregon to chop trees, he was able to make a cash offer that the man took on a handshake so he could get out of there sooner.

Oskar was only interested in it being a horse breeding farm with mostly pastures and paddocks. He only planted enough acres of oats to feed the horses. He became well known because he was honest and had big, strong, healthy horses. He spent his time breaking the young horses to the harness and sold them as ready-to-work draft horses.

After the third year, nobody was surprised when Oskar announced he was going back to Tranquil, Minnesota to marry the woman he'd been wooing by mail. They were going to have the wedding in two weeks and then come back to his farm. Everyone was invited to the wedding but couldn't afford railroad tickets or time away from the farm. They did arrange for a nice reception when the newlyweds returned. Theodora was a nice, slightly plump, cheerful, and hardworking young woman from a good family. They were strong and worked well together.

Manfred was not subtle when asking if she had any sisters or cousins or friends who might be inclined to come up and marry a hardworking bachelor farmer. Theodora said, "You are a good man and a wife would be treated well with you. I will ask but I can make no promises." She smiled at her new husband. "It took Oskar three years to convince me to marry him and come up here. I knew him before and saw him a few times each year when he came down to trade horses."

They didn't talk of it much more because there was so much summer and fall work to be done. They helped each other out quite a bit and Manfred loved eating good meals with them whenever there was a chance. He was not a pest but he had the charm and appreciation that the farmwives for miles around liked and kept inviting him to dinner or supper.

CHAPTER 12
Looking for Love

When winter set in, Manfred went to visit Oskar and Theodora one evening after supper. "Too late for supper tonight," she teased. "I need to eat on time to feed the new young'un on the way." That was the first anyone else knew that they had a child coming. "Sit down at the table. I have hot coffee and some of those newfangled tollhouse chocolate chip cookies if you'd like." Manfred was sitting at the table before she finished the sentence.

"Call Manfred anything you want but don't call him late for cookies," Oskar chuckled.

As they drank their coffee and ate cookies, Manfred said, "Oskar, isn't it time that I went down to visit Hilda? She's probably lonesome for me." He smiled at Theodora and added, "If there are so many lovely ladies back there as you say, I'd even get my hair cut and wear new clothes that I have coming from Sears Roebuck so I wouldn't embarrass anyone. I speak good English now since Miss Sorenson made me work at it so hard."

Theodora laughed and said to her husband, "He sure is determined and he might be right. No girl wants to buy a pig in a poke." With a wink, she added, "He is sort of handsome. Can he dance?"

"Ya sure, I dance!" Manfred crowed. "Schottische, polka, and I'll waltz their shoes off if they want!"

Oskar knew where this was going and had to tease a bit, "Maybe we'll go in a year or two."

Manfred's face fell but when Oskar and Theodora laughed, he realized they were joking. Oskar said, "I'm thinking we will be done with the hay around the first week of November. That would give me time to get there, trade some horses, and bring them back before Thanksgiving." He peered at Manfred, "Would you like to come with and ride back in the stock car with the new horses if I can get them?"

"Ya! I pack tomorrow."

"No need to rush, it's almost a month away. We have plenty of time."

Without saying anything to the men, Theodora conferred with Anna and some of the other wives who had come from Tranquil. They helped her compose letters to some young single women about maybe attending the harvest dance being held during the time Manfred and Oskar would be there. She hinted about a handsome friend who was a terrific dancer who might be there. Within the next few weeks she got a couple of interested responses.

She did not tell Oskar a thing about it, but the day she packed his old carpet bag for the trip she said, "Here. Take your good shoes and those blue pants and the red checkered shirt that came from the catalog last week."

"Why? I never brought fancy clothes before. We're not staying there for Thanksgiving."

"No, but you have to escort Manfred to the harvest dance at the Grange Hall the night after you get there."

"I don't want to go to a dance without you. You know I'm not the best dancer."

Theodora laughed. "My toes were bruised for a week after our wedding dance. Best you don't dance with anyone. You are there to make sure Manfred meets some ladies. Jane Larsen, Betsy Langmuir, Frieda Morgenstern, and a few others might be there expecting to meet him."

"How would you know that? I can barely remember who they are. I didn't know there was going to be a dance."

"Don't you make no never mind. It's just business for us women. You make sure you don't let Manfred get drunk and you don't either because I will hear about it."

"Yes, dear." Then after a pause he said, "Is there anything else I need to know?"

"Tell Manfred to bring his best clothes and shoes he can dance in," she said with a wink. "But don't tell him anything about who might be there." Oskar nodded, wondering when his wife had conjured this up.

#

Two nights later, the men caught the train going east through Minneapolis and then down home. Manfred was excited but didn't ask too many questions about the dance after Theodora gave him the fisheye. Oskar's father and Uncle John met them at the train. After introductions were made they went to look at Hilda. Manfred was delighted with her condition. She still had scars on her legs but they were well healed. "We keep socks on her in the winter," John said. Manfred was rubbing her nose as she nuzzled her old friend. "She's a good mare," John said. "Drops good foals and takes good care of them. She's a good mama." Manfred smiled broadly.

They went to Oskar's parents' house where his mother eagerly waited. Manfred was introduced and she liked him right away. She had coffee and rhubarb crisp for them. When Manfred asked for the recipe, she was totally smitten.

They had not slept well in the railroad passenger seats, so they went to bed because they'd have a full day tomorrow dealing with horses. "Hang up your good clothes so the wrinkles hang out," his mother said. Manfred was a little mystified as to how she knew he had new clothes with him but he was too tired to think about it.

The next morning, they had a great breakfast of ham, hash browns, eggs, toast, and coffee which Manfred thoroughly enjoyed. They went to three farms a few miles apart to look at some workhorses, did some bargaining, and promised to be back the next day. When they got back, Oskar's mother had a terrific supper ready of lamb chops, mashed potatoes, and all the fixings.

"Ma, you don't usually cook this much for me when I come back," Oskar said.

"You have a wife to cook for you but this handsome fellow doesn't," she said as she cleared the table. "Now you two get washed up and get on your new duds. The Grange Hall dance starts at seven o'clock and you're going to be on time. Pa and I are going, too."

Oskar was surprised, he'd only seen his folks at one dance and that was at his wedding. When he went to put on his good clothes, they had been ironed and his shoes had been polished. Oskar realized that his wife's conspiracies had spread as far as Minnesota.

#

They took the surrey and arrived right at seven o'clock as the band started their first tune. There were quite a few women, young and old, who seemed to be watching them. They sat on chairs at the edge of the dance floor. Manfred was tapping his foot to a peppy waltz.

One of Ma's friends came walking by and stopped to chat. Ma introduced Mrs. Larsen to Manfred and from out of nowhere, her auburn-haired daughter appeared. "This is my daughter, Jane," Mrs. Larsen said to Manfred. Then she added, "Jane, you know

Oskar. This is his North Dakota neighbor, Manfred." Manfred smiled and nodded.

"Does Manfred dance," Jane asked softly. "They're starting a polka." Manfred sprang to his feet, practically bowing, and offered his arm to her. In a fraction of a second they were on the dance floor and Manfred was leading her in a vigorous polka that had the two of them smiling and laughing. They talked as they danced a two-step and a waltz.

Jane's mother waived for them to come back. "Jane, thank the young man. We need to go talk to your aunt and uncle."

Jane looked disappointed but said, "Manfred, you are the best dancer I've ever been with. Maybe we can dance more later?" Before he could reply, she was whisked away by her mother.

Oskar handed Manfred a bottle of soda pop. Surprised, Manfred said hopefully, "Uh, I see they have beer."

"Not tonight," Ma said firmly. The young men were a little puzzled, but no one argued. After the next dance, another couple walked up and were introduced to Manfred. From behind them their daughter, a young, slender, blonde woman, appeared. In German she said, "I'm Frieda. I hear you came from the Fatherland. Do you like North Dakota?"

Manfred's eyes popped open wide as he jumped to his feet. "Ya, sure do," he said in German, then switched to English. "They are starting a schottische, do you know that dance?" Frieda nodded with enthusiasm and took his arm. They went out and had a good time. They also danced two waltzes and the "Beer Barrel Polka". Her parents pointed to some relatives to visit with. Frieda was reluctant to leave the dance floor but they were not to be reckoned with. She squeezed his hand before going with her parents.

Oskar was beginning to see the plot that his wife had set up to find a wife for Manfred. Manfred, however, was oblivious, grinning from ear-to-ear, and sweated up from dancing. He drank his soda practically in one gulp. "I'm thirsty," Manfred declared. "I'll buy you all another."

The two men went to the corner where the drinks were kept cool in a water tank. He offered up a dime and the kid selling the sodas said, "Nickel each or three for a dime." Manfred held up three fingers, not wanting to pass up a good deal. When he turned around, Oskar was talking to a young brunette.

"Manfred, this is Betsy, a neighbor of ours."

Manfred nodded, "Nice to meet you, Betsy. Would you care for a soda?" She smiled and accepted. The three of them went to Oskar's folks where they were talking to some more friends just as the band declared a break. They had a nice fact-finding conversation such as how they liked farming way up there by Canada and so forth.

When the band started up again, Betsy was tapping her foot in time to the music. Oskar gave Manfred a little shove and jerked his head toward the dance floor.

Manfred quickly caught on and politely said, "Miss, would you care to try this waltz?" As soon as they set their sodas down, they were out dancing. They had a lot of fun and she was enjoying such a strong leader on the dance floor. Many women seemed to be watching him.

When they went back to the chairs, the bandleader called out, "Ladies' choice." Before Manfred could ask what that was, a young woman with curly red hair grabbed his hand and dragged him out on the dance floor for a two-step. They danced and then another woman cut in for the next one and another for the next.

Oskar rescued Manfred for little rest and a sip of soda. After the next break, Manfred danced with Jane, Frieda, and Betsy a few more times. He had a big smile but was also looking a little bit bewildered. "Oskar, I feel like a horse in a field of clover. I don't know where to turn next."

Oskar slapped him on the back and said with a chuckle, "Enjoy it while you can my friend. We leave on the train tomorrow after midnight." At eleven o'clock the band called it quits and Manfred had his hands full saying thank you and goodbye to about half-a-dozen young women who were smiling and chatting with him.

On the way home, Ma asked, "Manfred, did you meet anyone you liked tonight?"

"Oh ya! I like them all. I wonder if any of them liked me?" The others burst out laughing, almost startling the horse.

#

In the morning they went back to two of the farms and finalized the deal for three teams to take up to North Dakota later that night. It went quick and when they got back to the house for midmorning coffee, Ma said, "Wash the horse smell off and put on your good duds again." The boys looked curious. "The Morgensterns have invited us over for noon dinner."

"Frieda's parents?" Manfred asked. Ma nodded and saw he was smiling.

They went two doors down to a well-kept clapboard house and had a very nice beef roast with carrots and potatoes. Mrs. Morgenstern made sure everyone knew that Frieda had made all the food on her own including baking German rye bread this morning. Frieda had her hair in a long blonde braid down her back. "She sewed her dress and apron, too," Mrs. Morgenstern said.

It was obvious to everyone except Manfred that they were touting their daughter's homemaking skills. After delicious apple streusel for dessert, they had to say goodbye. Manfred was startled when Frieda gave him a hug.

Back at the house, Manfred and Oskar were going up to change back into their work clothes when Ma said that some friends were coming for coffee. At three o'clock who should show up but the Langmuirs and daughter Betsy wearing a very nice dress and fancy apron, her long brown hair up in a neat bun. They sat and talked a lot about farming on the prairie.

Mr. Langmuir asked many questions about what was up in Northfield, North Dakota, and how many cows and horses he had. Mrs. Langmuir was curious about how big a house he had. It was hard for Manfred to concentrate on the questions with Betsy sitting next to him, much closer than necessary. She smelled like vanilla. She was telling him how much she had enjoyed the dancing last night and how she would like to do that again. Then as it was near time for them to go, she slipped her hand under the table to squeeze his hand and held it warmly until they had to get up. They said their goodbyes with Manfred smiling broadly again.

Back at the house, they donned their work clothes, packed their bags along with the rhubarb crisp recipe from Ma tucked in and letters to everyone up there. After all, why pay for postage stamps when they had personal delivery?

Ma said she would bring their bags to the train later. They got the horses, drove them into the railroad corrals, and paid the railroad stock car fee. Then they went back for a nice supper with Ma and Pa. Ma gave them another old thick wool quilt because the open stock car would be cold in the November weather. Pa gave them a tarp to help keep the wind off also.

Back at the stockyard, Oskar's father and uncle helped load the horses who were skittish getting into a train car for the first time. There was a little kicking and one mare nipped Manfred.

Ma came out in the surrey but had someone with her. To Manfred's surprise it was Jane Larsen with her own big basket of food for their long trip back north. He noticed her pretty auburn hair peeking out from under a colorful headscarf. They didn't have much time but she said she hoped he would come back and visit soon. She would write to him since she now knew where to send it. She gave him a quick hug then Ma escorted her back home in the surrey.

As they shook hands with Pa, he said with a grin, "Pleasure to meet you Manfred, we will probably be seeing you again before long." Manfred smiled and nodded but totally missed the innuendo. There was no more time for talk as the train was pulling out. They threw their bags and bundles in and climbed up into the rail car with the horses as the train men shut the doors. The train chugged into the dark moonless night. Once the horses were settled down, they nestled into the straw in the most sheltered part of the car under a tarp and the quilt, bundled up in their heavy winter coats, hats, and long- johns.

It was a long, cold ride north but the food basket from Jane was a delight. "She must have been cooking and baking all day," Manfred said in wonderment.

When they got home the next night and unloaded the horses, Harold was there with the wagon. They loaded everything and put the horses on long leads to trail home. Theodora was up when Oskar got home. She raised her eyebrows questioningly.

"The man charmed half the women back home and danced their feet off," Oskar said to her delight. "I think three of them would have loaded up with the horses if he had suggested it."

She laughed and clapped her hands with glee. "We'll see if anything comes of it. It's going to be a long winter."

#

Within a week, Manfred had letters from Jane, Betsy, Frieda, and two other women whose faces he didn't remember. Their letters were all friendly, full of praise, and many polite questions about his life and farm. They didn't come right out and ask his intentions but almost. The problem was that after waiting and hoping to meet a woman for most of four years with no prospects, he suddenly had a choice of three lovely women and maybe two more if he could remember who they were. He would have chosen any one of them a week ago but now he didn't know what to do. He decided to ask Anna and Theodora for advice.

Two weeks later, Theodora and Anna took the wagon to town to pick up some supplies that they needed for the upcoming winter. When they were at the depot looking for their mail and packages from Sears, Theodora gave Anna a poke in the side. In a whisper she said, "Isn't that the Mannheim girl from Tranquil sitting over there?"

Anna looked and said, "Is it? I guess so, but she was such a gawky young girl last time I saw her."

They stepped closer, "Debra? Is that you?" Theodora asked.

CHAPTER 13
The Farmer takes a Wife

Debra jumped up and hugged them. "I came on the train late last night." She looked a little sheepish. "I didn't know where your farms were. I was waiting to ask somebody. I think I fell asleep in this chair." She became quiet. The confused wives were unsure how to ask what she was doing there uninvited.

"Hey, ho! Missus!" Three men came rushing up to them whom Anna quickly recognized. "We just loaded out a hunnert bushel of wheat," Ivar said. "It's going to the mill back east."

Anna stood up, "Nice to see you Johnson boys. Where's Karl?"

"He got a cold so he stayed home," Bernt said. "Who're these ladies?"

"This is Oskar's wife Theodora and their baby Bjorn, and this is Miss Mannheim, just come in from our hometown in Minnesota." They all shook hands and the Johnson brothers took turns admiring the baby swaddled up in heavy blankets.

Turning his attention to Debra, Lars asked, "Miss, are you going to be their milkmaid?"

"Oh, I don't know, maybe. Or I might find work in a store here," Debra said as she looked the three handsome men over.

"We need a cook. We can pay good, too," Lars offered. "Our cook got married and left."

"Oh, I don't know if that would be proper for a young lady to live unchaperoned on a farm with four single men," Anna interjected.

"I kept house and cooked for the Hiller brothers back home. Mother said I did a good job," Debra said. She looked Anna and Theodora in the eyes. "I'm not afraid of men. I know how to handle them."

"Well, we'd better talk this out some more, but not here. Why don't all four of you boys come over for noon dinner on Sunday," Anna said. "Debra, find your bags and we'll bring the wagon around back." When they pulled the wagon up to the platform, Debra was standing there with a big trunk, two canvas cases, and a wood crate as big as the trunk. The Johnson brothers were chatting with her, smiling and nodding. The men grabbed her baggage and loaded it with easy effort. Two of them helped Debra mount up on the wagon seat. Anna shook the reins to get started. "See you boys Sunday." They all waved goodbye, grinning until they turned the corner out of sight.

"Debra, um, does your mother know you're up here?" Theodora asked. She knew Debra was very impulsive.

"Oh, yes. I left her a note with your names on it before I left. I was at the dance where your handsome husband and that good-looking Manfred were at. I danced with Manfred." They were quiet for a bit as they bumped along on the prairie trail on the way home. Debra was smiley and almost bouncing with excitement, "Is all the farmland this rich?"

"Mostly. Do you really want to work in a store or keep house for a bunch of men?" Theodora said. "How old are you?"

"I'm twenty-four, an old maid already my mother says. I heard some of the girls talking, they said there were lots of men up here looking for wives." Taking a deep breath, she asked, "Is that true? Could an old maid like me find a husband around here?"

Anna and Theodora started laughing. "Debra, you could be married a dozen times before Sunday if you stood in town with a sign around your neck saying, Husband Wanted."

"Really? Better than those Johnson brothers even?"

"Oh, I don't know if there are better ones than them, but maybe." Anna said.

"You can stay with Oskar and me for a while. You can help with the baby and the milking."

"Can I? That would be wonderful."

It started to snow big fluffy flakes before they got home. "Hope you brought a heavy coat and boots," Anna said.

"Oh yes, and my grandma's old fur hat and full-length beaver coat, too."

Anna stopped at Oskar and Theodora's house. When Oskar came out to help with the supplies he was startled to see Debra. He knew who she was but hadn't talked to her except to say hello for years. He was a little dubious when he and Theodora went in the house and she told him that Debra would stay with them for a while, until they could get her settled someplace.

"I saw her grab Manfred for one dance. She didn't come up here thinking she'd marry him, did she?"

"I don't know. I'm not sure if she even knows. She sure was flirting with the Johnson boys at the depot." As they unloaded the wagon she said, "We're going to Anna's for Sunday dinner and the Johnsons are going to be there."

"My God. This is too fast for my head," Oskar laughed.

#

Theodora told Anna she would bring three rhubarb pies on Sunday. Anna nodded and waved goodbye, anxious to get home before the snow got heavier and to tell Harold the news about Debra. It was a short mile to their home but the snow got heavier until she almost couldn't see the place. Luckily all she had to do was follow the fence line. Harold heard her coming and unhooked the team while she took the supplies into the house. She kicked off her boots, shook the snow off her coat and headscarf before hanging them on the pegs by the door.

Harold had the boys put the horses in the barn, curry comb them, and feed them some oats. He came in as Anna was putting a bag of flour in the tight barrel so the mice wouldn't get into it. "Anything new in town?"

Anna sat down at the table, leaned back in her chair and put her hands over her face. "Oh, my goodness. You have no idea." She told him about Debra, the Johnson boys, and all.

"She just packed everything, bought a train ticket, and only left her mother a note?" Harold asked incredulously. Anna nodded. "And the Johnson brothers are coming for noon dinner Sunday? They want to hire her?" Anna kept nodding. "You'd better write a letter to her mother to let her know where she ended up. The poor woman must be worried out of her mind."

"I'll write tonight but with the snow we won't get it to the depot for days." That night she wrote the letter but didn't seal the envelope until she knew it would be sent. It snowed all night and through the day but the following morning was clear and totally brilliant with the sun shining on the new snow.

Oskar came skiing up fast. "Had to dig these out of the barn. Scrubbed some wax on and here I am." When he saw Anna wasn't close he quietly said, "Harold, what the hell is going on with this Debra girl?"

Harold shook his head, "You know as much as I do. Anna wrote a letter to Debra's mother to let her know she's here with us but we can't get it to the depot until I get the sled runners on the wagon box."

"I'll ski it into the depot today. The weather looks good for a while."

Harold got the letter which Anna sealed. Anna came out for a minute and said, "Thanks for taking the letter in. Do you have time to ski down to Johnsons' place and ask them what they have in mind about Debra. I've never seen their house. Is it fit for a woman to live in?"

#

Oskar ran on his skis to town. He could cover the five miles in a half hour. It took another hour to get to the Johnsons who were happy to see him. They fed him dinner that they were ready to eat: fried venison steaks, fried potatoes, and rye crisp with beer. It was good.

"What are you boys thinking about Debra? She's a little unsettled right now and staying with us for a while. She is good at milking and can cook. It helps Theodora but I don't need a full-time maid."

"Can one of us marry her?" Bernt asked in all seriousness.

"What? You mean like right now? You only just met her for maybe five minutes!"

"But she's nice and smiles a lot. She seemed to like us." The brothers were all frowning and asking why she couldn't marry one of them.

"Jeezey Pete! Now I've about heard it all," Oskar exclaimed. "How long have you guys been out here without a woman around?"

"Except for that old widow cook we had last year, that'd be most of five years," Lars said. "You wouldn't understand, you've got a wife and a baby. We ain't got anything close to that." The brothers were all nodding. "Besides why couldn't she marry us?"

"There you have it. You said it. She can't marry all of you."

"I'll marry her," they said in unison.

Shaking his head in disbelief, Oskar said, "You better talk it over before you get to Harold's on Sunday. You all sound completely nuts right now. If you want to scare this poor girl away you go ahead and talk like that when you get there." Oskar looked them over, "You're going to go up against the toughest judges of your lives on Sunday." The brothers looked puzzled. "Anna and Theodora and Harold and I are going to have to be totally convinced that this girl should even consider *any* of you."

He got up and put on his hat and coat. "Thanks for dinner, it was good. Oh, and don't tell anybody that you drink beer with dinner." Then he buckled on the long, wood, hog-nosed Norwegian

162

style cross country skis and ran across the fresh snow. He flew across the prairie and was home in an hour.

The next morning, Oskar and Theodora went to visit Harold and Anna leaving Debra home with the baby. They had coffee and talked about what might happen Sunday. "I'm afraid Debra's not the sharpest knife in the drawer," Oskar said frankly.

"She thinks she knows men but I'm thinking she's more than naive. Might be she doesn't really know the facts of life. Her family is pretty prudish and probably never talked to her about those things," Theodora said.

"The Johnsons are pretty desperate after five years out here. They need a woman around. Given a choice, every one of them would marry her. If there were four girls ready they would marry them in a heartbeat, probably sight unseen! Maybe they'll draw straws or something."

"Let's not tell Debra any of this. Just wait until Sunday and see what shakes out," Harold advised.

Once that was agreed upon, everybody went back to work. There were sleds that needed snow runners fitted up. Harold took one team to the blacksmith and had them sharp-shod so they could run on ice. The sharp-shod horseshoes had point spikes on the bottom that kept them from slipping and falling on ice.

When the lake froze over they would be able to travel the fifteen miles down to a bigger town on the lake to the south or they could go up into Canada. Winter made travel a lot faster as long as they kept an eye on the weather and storms. There were always people who got caught out in the snow, got lost, or weren't prepared when the temperatures plummeted to forty below zero overnight. Sometimes they wouldn't find the bodies until spring when the snowbanks melted.

The kids were excited that the Johnson brothers were coming. They thought they'd bring more toys like they did before. It felt like a holiday even though Thanksgiving was still a week away. The Johnsons were almost unrecognizable when they arrived in their jingling sleigh pulled by a team of golden draft horses with manes and tails brushed and braided. The sleigh must have had fifty bells on it and more on the horses' harnesses. Every one of them was shaved clean and their hair was cut by someone who knew what he was doing.

As they alighted from the sleigh, Harold and Anna smelled Bay Rum hair tonic. The young men's clothes looked brand-new, all smooth with creases in place. Each of them wore a nice string tie and they put on dressy shoes that they had carried in their coat pockets after they pulled off their fur-lined boots. Lars sported a luxurious raccoon coat with matching fur hat.

Debra was wearing her good gray wool dress and a green apron. She looked very nice and was not a bit nervous as she had no idea what this was all about. The brothers all looked nervous and acted as though they had practiced their manners and actions.

The kids looked at them curiously. These didn't seem like the boisterous jolly men who came after Christmas last year. They quickly lost interest when they realized they were not the focus of the visit and there were no presents for them.

Anna had prepared a nice dinner of venison roast, carrots, mashed potatoes, and spicy pickled crabapples. Theodora's rhubarb pie with clotted cream topping was a big hit. When the kids were excused from the table to go play, the grownups sat sipping coffee.

Lars Johnson, the eldest at thirty-five, was the accepted head of the Johnson brothers. Every farm needed a boss and he was it. Sitting very erect, he began, "Miss Mannheim, we did not mean anything too forward when we met you in town earlier this week." He pointed to his brothers. "We are all decently raised men who respected our parents before their passing back in Norway. We can all read, write, and do arithmetic. Anyone who knows us will tell you that we are hardworking, moral men."

Debra was a bit wide-eyed at his speech. She looked at each of the brothers for a clue as to what was happening here. The married couples sat back, their attention on the performance in front of them. The brothers were looking at her intently and obviously expected some sort of a reply, so she started out softly, "You all seem like nice men." She looked at each one and smiled as she said, "Please, call me Debra."

"We did not want you to think what we are going to ask is sinful or whorish," Lars continued. That got a reaction from the wives and stern looks from Harold and Oskar. Realizing his error, Lars plowed ahead, "What I'm trying to say is that if you would want to come visit our house and get to know us better, you would be more than welcome."

"I guess that would be okay. Are you saying you don't want me to come cook for you?" She looked a little disappointed and confused. "Should I get a job in town someplace?"

Anna spoke up, "Debra, we don't want you to bring any question on your reputation. You've had a proper upbringing but living with a bunch of men without a mother to keep an eye on things might not look good."

"My mother's been calling me an old maid. I ain't going be no old maid. That's worse than a bad reputation." She took a deep breath. "As wonderful as you all are, I do not plan to live out here on Oskar or Harold's farm. You are fine people, but I came out here to start my own life."

Looking somewhat relieved, Lars plunged ahead, "We have a job to offer. We want to invite all of you and, of course, Manfred to our place for Thanksgiving dinner if Debra would agree to come and do the cooking. She could see us and all we have and it would be proper."

Anna said, "It's a week from Thursday, you know."

Before anyone else could say anything, Debra said emphatically, "Yes! I'll work up a list of groceries for you to buy. Anna, Theodora, would you help me with the recipes and ingredients?" They both nodded.

Smiling broadly, Lars said, "We will pay you to do the cooking and we will pay you more if you will also do the cleaning." He reached into his pocket and pulled out a wad of money. "We would like you to do the grocery shopping, too." He placed the whole wad of cash in front of Debra.

She did not touch the money. "Yes, I will cook Thanksgiving dinner. I will buy your groceries, but I need to clean the house first and see what spices, dinnerware, and supplies you have." The four brothers leaned back in their chairs with pleased expressions. Debra took a deep breath as everyone looked at her. "One more thing," she said.

"Yes, Miss, what would that be?"

"Do you have a turkey?"

"No, I mean yes we did, but a fox got it," Bernt said. "You pick one and we'll buy it."

Anna spoke up, "This sounds like a real feast. We'd be happy to come. It will be nice not having to cook for a change."

Theodora added, "We will be there with bells on. Are you thinking of eating at two or three o'clock?"

Debra said, "Three. I have to check their oven first."

Ivar blurted, "Oven?"

"I didn't see any oven when I was there," Oskar said. "I did see a cooktop coal stove though."

Lars quickly said, "You will have an oven and a good stove so do not worry." A few of the brothers' eyebrows went up. Anna thought: *I might end up cooking Thanksgiving dinner after all.*

Feeling more confident, Debra said, "Come and get me a week from Monday at sunrise. I will spend the day cleaning and making a list of essential things like food, dishes, kettles, and such." No one spoke, so she continued, "I will shop for groceries and a turkey on Tuesday but one of you will have to take me to town. Pick me up at sunrise on Wednesday so I can get the table ready for dinner. On Thursday, I'll need to be picked up by three o'clock in the morning so I can get all of the cooking and serving ready for people to come at two o'clock and eat at three."

"Yes! Yes!" Lars cried, "One of us will be at Oskar's door at sunrise those days and at three Thanksgiving morning." All the boys stood up. Each one gave his thanks to Anna for the meal. Lars said, "Thank you for accepting our invitation for Thanksgiving and to Debra for agreeing to be the lady of the house that day."

The brothers politely shook hands and then headed home in their sleigh. In the silence of the winter snow when they went out to hitch the horse to Oskar's sleigh, they could hear the Johnson brothers arguing even a half-mile away. "I hope they can put their money where their mouths are," was all Harold said.

Oskar shook his head and barked out a short laugh, "They don't have a real cook stove or an oven. How can they get one this quick? Besides there's no extra room for both their coal heater and a real cooking range or everybody at the same time. It's a pretty small place."

"We'll have to wait and see. Ask Debra when she gets back after her first day there. It would be easier if she stayed there but Anna won't allow that. Wouldn't be proper."

#

Early Monday morning, a tired looking Karl was at the door in his sleigh at sunrise as promised. "We have to go to town on the way home to buy a few things if that's good for you."

Debra nodded but wondered what they would be buying. As they went into the dry goods store, Karl said, "You pick out every cleaning thing you think you might need and make sure you have something to clean an oven with."

"But you don't have an oven, do you?"

Karl squinted at the clock on the wall but did not reply. He went in the back with the shop owner and they started carrying out boxes and Debra's hastily selected cleaning products to put in the back of the sleigh. Karl paid for everything from another big wad of cash. Just as they were going out of the store, he looked at the wall clock and smiled. With a wink he said, "Yes, we now have an oven." Under his breath he muttered, "At least I sure hope so."

Debra did not understand but they loaded up and were at the Johnson homestead in half an hour. One of the boys was up on the roof and waved at them as they pulled into the yard next to the door. Karl waved and hollered, "Well?"

Lars stepped out of the house and hollered back, "Yes."

"Yes, what?" Debra asked.

"You'll see," Karl said with a grin.

They went into the house and what Debra saw mostly dismayed her. The coal heater with a coffee pot on top was glowing. They had a real wood floor which was a nice surprise. They made three trips carrying cleaning supplies, brooms, mop, soap, scrub brushes, and Murphy's Oil soap inside. Karl and Bernt carried the mysterious boxes around back and she could hear the other two up on the roof.

"I'm going to start cleaning," she said, "but I don't think I can cook a turkey here without an oven."

"Don't worry. We have it. We'll show it to you when you are done cleaning."

There was a lot of banging and some cursing coming through the wall as the next few hours went by. Debra got busy cleaning. From time to time, one or two of the boys would come in measuring with a carpenter's ruler. She was curious but didn't say anything.

When Lars came back in about noon he looked around. "This room has never been cleaner. Now will you please clean the two bedrooms?" He pointed to the doors and opened them to reveal a full iron bed in each one with clothes hanging on wall pegs. She carried her mop bucket and broom in and started cleaning. For a bunch of men living here for five years it was pretty clean.

When she was finishing the second bedroom, she heard lots of hammering and sawing. There was more cursing and grunting. "Debra please wait a minute," Lars said through the door of the bedroom that she had closed to keep the dust from getting in. After hearing some boots scuffling and whispers, Lars said, "Come out please."

She stepped out, looked at Lars, and then over to where two of the brothers were standing grinning. She almost fell over when she looked past the brothers and didn't see the wall that had been there when she arrived. She was looking into a new, shack-sized room. It was empty except for a table, chairs, and a big cast iron range with a large oven and two warming ovens above. Dark blue stovepipes went out through the ceiling. There was another door and a window on the opposite wall.

"W-w-what the hell?" she blurted. The brothers burst out laughing as she turned bright red.

Lars took her by the arm and stepped her over a new wood threshold that ran the length of where the old wall had been. He hollered out the open door, "Bernt, is it ready?"

"Yes, light it up!"

Lars pulled a blue-tip wood match from his pocket and handed it to Debra. He opened the top of the fire box which was already filled with crumpled paper, sticks, and some coal to the side. She stepped forward, striking the match on the cast iron top. In a few minutes, the fire was going and they closed up the top.

"Open the damper more, she's smoking too much," Ivar hollered from outside. Debra was used to iron ranges and had it adjusted and burning nicely in a few minutes. All the boys gathered together grinning with satisfaction.

"Do you like it," Karl asked. "We got it for you."

"How did you do all this so fast?"

"There was a New Yorker on the next quarter who took off on the train last week. He'd given up trying to make it here, couldn't stand the isolation. We bought up his land which had this one-room wood shack with the range and the big table and chairs in it," Lars said proudly.

172

"There was a bed but we think it had bedbugs so we threw it outside," Karl explained. "We pulled the shack over with three teams of horses. We cut off this end of the wall and nailed it to our house. The chimney pipes were rusty so that's what I was buying in the store, along with a damper and a rain cap." They closed the outside door and the new kitchen started to heat it up fast.

"I don't know what to say," Debra said. "Never heard the like before. That's a real nice range. It has a hot water well, warming compartments, and an enormous oven. It even has a thermometer in the door. Wow. I better get busy cleaning this new addition," Debra said. She looked in the oven, "Not that bad, don't think he baked much."

She lifted all the flat top pieces and used a little broom to sweep the ash into the fire box. The ash pan below had been emptied so she shook the grate and then added more coal from the bucket that one of the boys brought in. "Can you bring in a couple of buckets of good water to put in the hot water well? It doesn't look like it's ever been used. With this you will have hot water all the time the stove is lit. That's a real luxury." She was smiling which encouraged the men to work even harder.

One of them poured water into the stove well. They all looked but couldn't see any water or smoke leaks. Satisfied that they had done everything possible for now inside the house, the men went out and started working on the roof and the walls where it joined together. Soon there were no drafts coming through the cracks.

#

Debra started sweeping and knocking down cobwebs. There was a lot of dust because the shaking and dragging of the shack knocked plenty of dirt loose. It swept up easily. This part had an even better wood floor. She noticed a door in the back corner of the room. Afraid of what might be in there, she opened it cautiously. No critters leaped out at her which was a relief. When she got the door wide open she saw shelves. To her amazement, it was a closet.

She reached in with a rag around her hands and started pulling out the contents. She had the boys bring the long wood table over closer. When the closet was empty, she looked at the full table. There was every type of cast iron pot, pan, kettle, and a gigantic roaster. It was apparent that only the frying pan and a couple of the smallest cooking pots and coffee pot had ever been used.

There was a large galvanized zinc wash pan with the paper label still on it. In the bottom was the receipt from Sears for $7.77 for the Acme iron cookware set. Debra was grinning ear-to-ear. She set the big wash pan on the stovetop and poured in water to warm up.

While the dishwater was heating, she swept the closet and washed it out so she could put the items back in when she had them cleaned up. She carried every piece of cookware, dinnerware, and silverware in from the existing cooking area. Some pots needed lots of soaking and scrubbing. It took a couple of hours and she about wore out the new scrub brush. The new towels were all used and wet by the time she was done.

The boys kept popping in to see what she discovered. They had forgotten to eat at noon because they were so busy. When she had the table cleared and cookware stored in the closet, she put away the plates, and cooked a fresh pot of coffee. Taking a steel ladle to bang on the biggest pot lid, she called them in to sit at the new table.

They had coffee, rye crisp, cheese, and cold sausages with mustard. It wasn't much but she surmised that they probably ate like that often. The brothers were all grins and compliments, even liking how she served the rye crisp and cheese.

"What more shall we do here before Thanksgiving?" Lars asked.

"Move your other small table and chairs in here," Debra said. Before she finished the sentence, they had hauled it all in. The old table was over an inch taller than the long table but it was the same width on the end. In an instant, the brothers had sawed the legs down so they matched after some whittling. Debra was amazed. "Nice job boys. Do you have a tablecloth?" That only got dumb looks and negative head shakes.

"I saw one of you had a carpenter's rule," she said. "Put the tables together and measure them up apart and then together. Together they might be big enough to squeeze everybody around but there are only seven chairs. We'll have to get a big tablecloth."

"I'll make benches," Bernt volunteered.

"Can you bring in that old sideboard?"

"That was our mother's from her mother. It's oak," Ivar said as he and Karl carried it into the big room.

"Yes, I know. I cleaned it up. Its beautifully carved." It fit well in the room. "Remember to keep adding water to the hot well on the stove as you take it out. Don't run out of hot water. It'll make life easier."

Lars came in carrying something. "I got this figured out," he bragged. "It's a kerosene ceiling lamp for over the table." It was chrome with a fancy glass shade. It gleamed after Debra washed it up. They mounted it in the ceiling where she suggested so it shed more light on the stove. She was getting pretty good at giving orders to the men.

It was getting close to dark when they gave her a fast sleigh ride home. She was a very tired girl who ate little at supper and then hit the mattress pad on the floor in the corner. She told Oskar and Theodora a little but was too exhausted to go into detail.

CHAPTER 14
Another Bachelor Bites the Dust

The next morning, Debra had oatmeal with the family. Theodora handed her the grocery list they had made up. She was ready to go when Ivar arrived with the sleigh. They went to town and bought a lot of kitchen things including two durable, green-checkered tablecloths and a set of nice but inexpensive china plates, bowls, and cups. Ivar insisted she pick out a set of silverware. She added to her list items that were missing from the Johnson house. She had opened their spice tins only to find most of them were empty. The sleigh was piled high with boxes.

They asked around town and finally found someone who had a big tom turkey for sale on a farm a couple of miles northwest. They brought the trussed, unhappy bird to their farm and put him in a part of the chicken coop where he wouldn't attack the hens. He settled down when they fed and watered him.

Debra cooked dinner on the stove for the delighted men. After more cleaning and arranging, she was almost satisfied. She had washed up the new dishes but they used the mishmash of old dishes for every day. Karl brought her home a little earlier this time and the next day she was there again baking and fussing all day. She made them a nice stew for dinner and cut one of her loaves of white bread fresh out of the oven.

The men were in heaven, happy, laughing, and joking. They were all comfortable with each other, it seemed like Debra could be a good fit for this crew. They took her home even earlier because Thursday was going to be an early and very long day. She knew she was going to be on trial in front of the families attending.

#

At three a.m. Thursday, she climbed bleary-eyed into the sleigh. She fell asleep under the heavy horsehide and felt sleigh blankets. When they reached the Johnsons' place, she was happy to see that the big turkey was ready for her, gutted, and plucked clean. She started fixing dressing to stuff the turkey, trussed it up, and got it in the oven.

They did not have a scale so they all guessed the weight between twenty to twenty-two pounds. It would take until two o'clock to get done. She loved the thermometer on the oven.

Debra prepared side dishes of yams, potatoes, scalloped corn, green bean casserole, and much more. The men kept begging for tastes but she shooed them away. It was a handsome bird. Lars brought in an enormous knife from the shop sharpened bright.

Three sleighs pulled in together at two o'clock. The brothers were busy greeting the guests and taking their coats to heap up on the beds as well as giving the men and boys a quick tour of the barns, bins, and shops. They opened the doors of the grain bins to show wheat and barley full-to-the-top ready to ship. They were just waiting for the prices to go up.

The children played in the other room while the babies took naps in a bedroom. Anna and Theodora offered to help but soon found that Debra had everything mostly done. There were some radishes and green onions to trim and carrot sticks to set out. Debra was busy showing them her new stove and telling the story of the new kitchen and dining table that the brothers had surprised her with. She had no time to turn away from the stove as they talked.

Lars lifted the big turkey out of the oven when Debra said it was time. He and Debra scooped out the stuffing. He set the big platter on the table and asked everyone to sit down. Debra was busy making gravy. When she turned to put it on the table and take her seat, she finally looked at them all.

Lars had to keep her from dropping the gravy boat because sitting at the other end of the table in their Sunday best were her mother and father.

#

She started to cry and rushed to hug them exclaiming, "When did you get here?" After hugs, her mother told her to sit down so they could say grace and the guests could start to eat. Stunned, she sat next to Lars who led them in prayer. He carved the turkey and they started passing around heaping bowls of everything.

Bernt went around the table pouring water for everyone saying, "Drink a lot of water. It will fill you up so you won't eat so much." He laughed the most at his joke.

After everyone's plate was filled, Debra asked, "Mother, how is it you came here now?"

"I found your note when I came home and you and your clothes were gone," Mrs. Mannheim said. "I was afraid you'd run off with that drummer selling brushes that week."

"Oh, Mother! I wouldn't do that."

"You did not say where you were going, I was frantic until I got a nice letter from Anna." Debra's head swiveled to look at Anna. Anna just smiled and kept eating. "So, I told Papa that we would go to see where you were going to settle your life. I sent Anna a letter telling her the first train we could come on. They picked us up from the train this morning." She nodded at everyone around the table. "Debra surprised us so now we surprised her." Manfred and the brothers laughed at the great joke. "But the joke is on Papa and me because our Debra has made a meal I could never have managed alone, and in a stranger's kitchen to boot."

Flushed with pleasure, Debra left the table to whip the cream for the pies as everybody chattered and laughed. It was a wonderful Thanksgiving for new and old friends and family. "Apple or pumpkin," she asked as she went around the table.

Manfred and Bernt wanted one of each. They passed the whipped cream to help themselves as Debra poured coffee.

Bernt said, "Do you like these new dishes? Debra picked them out and the silverware and the tablecloths and most everything that is good here. She really spruced the place up."

"Debra! You cannot spend these men's money so lavishly. All new plates, silverware, and such, it's more than I've ever had my whole life," her mother admonished.

Lars spoke up, "Mrs. Mannheim, we asked her to get it for us. We wouldn't have any idea of what or how to get the right things. Debra must have learned her good taste from you."

Debra's mother blushed at that but did not give up, "Debra, it is too much money of theirs you've spent! It's not yours!"

Bernt chimed in, "Don't you worry none. We've brought in four crops now and have sold more wheat than we can count and made good money at it. It was time we spent some of it and we are glad that you are all here to enjoy it with us."

Debra's father was hard of hearing but refused to use the ear trumpet the doctor gave him. He usually sat in the middle of conversations nodding his head saying, "Ya, ya" from time to time. Of course, his family knew he wasn't hearing much of anything but they did not want to hurt his pride by repeating things to him.

While they were drinking more coffee and talking about wheat prices, acreage, bushels per acre, calves, and horses, Debra's father leaned toward Lars and asked loudly, "When did you say the wedding is?"

The table went silent. Debra turned bright red and her mother shook her head no at Pa. "What?" he shouted. "Can't I even ask my future son-in-law when the happy day will be?" He looked a little angry and confused.

Lars was blushing too, and Debra couldn't look him in the eye. The others were grinning, barely able to subdue their laughter. "Hey Lars," Bernt said. "When is the wedding?" Lars could not answer.

Debra stood up, her face flaming. "Father," she said loud enough for him to hear. "He has not asked me yet!" There was a short, uncomfortable silence. She startled them all when she said, "But if he would, I would say yes to any day he chose." When she sat down, Lars gaped at her in astonishment and the rest gazed upon her as if she'd sprouted angel's wings and a halo.

Lars stood up awkwardly and took hold of Debra's hand. Clearing his throat, he said, "If you mean that, then I say now." With a little gasp, Debra nodded her head as tears streamed down her cheeks. Lars's brothers whooped and hollered, the men got up and shook his hand while the women clustered around Debra, everyone hugging and crying. The kids were so confused.

Debra's father shouted, "Well it better be danged quick! Our train ticket home is Monday. We didn't come here just for Thanksgiving, did we?"

Bernt said, "Sunday would be good. We will set a time in the town church and pay a preacher. Maybe at noon when services are done?"

Debra turned her face to Lars and whispered, "Do you really mean it?" Choked with emotion, he could only nod. "Then my answer is yes and Sunday is perfect. I would like to have my parents here for my wedding."

Manfred started to clap and the rest joined in. "Kiss her you fool," he shouted and everyone laughed. The couple had never even held hands let alone kissed. It was very awkward for a first kiss in front of everyone. Debra looked him in the eye, tilting her head back, lips pursed a bit. He looked down into her eyes, quickly bent down, and kissed her firmly. They broke the briefest of kisses as everyone clapped more. She went around the table to kiss her mother and father and Lars followed shaking hands.

This would be a Thanksgiving to remember as shockingly as it all unfolded. Family stories about this would last for generations to come. The rest of the day went by in a swirl. Anna and Theodora kept glancing at Debra and Lars, smiling and shaking their heads in wonder.

After all the dishes were washed, they had more pie and coffee before everyone headed home to get the evening milking done. Debra and her parents were driven home by Lars in his big sleigh. This was a dream he could hardly believe. He kept looking at his soon-to-be bride sitting snuggled up to him. When they dropped her parents off at Harold's, he drove Debra to Oskar's.

"My father doesn't hear well," Debra said when they were alone in the sleigh. "He was confused. He must have thought I came up here for a wedding and since you were sitting at the head of the table, he figured it was you." When they stopped in front of the door she continued, "You don't have to marry me. Nobody has a shotgun in your back."

"Debra, I'm not sure how this all happened. If truth be told, I had been thinking that you are a fine woman to put up with my brothers and me. You cook good, too. I was hoping that maybe during the winter you would let me court you proper-like."

She gave a short laugh, "Well this has to be the shortest courtship ever." She looked him in the face again and said seriously, "But you really don't have to. I'll understand."

"I never said I didn't want to. I have never wanted anything more." He took a deep breath and said almost fearfully, "I'd understand if you want to wait a while so we can get to know each other better."

"I know you well enough. Not long, but enough. I'll marry you Sunday afternoon if you'll have me." His answer was to pull her close and kiss her warmly.

She reached up and kissed him back for a long time. They took a couple of breaths then kissed deeply again and then again. "Whew, Lars, maybe Sunday isn't soon enough." He laughed and so did she. He walked her to the door and they kissed good night. Their dreams of belonging to someone special were about to come true.

The next few days blew by getting ready for the wedding. The church and a preacher were secured. Debra had to find a suitable dress in the only store that had women's ready-to-wear. Lars had to find a suit. Of course, flowers were out of the question that time of year, so Theodora and Anna made tissue paper roses for her to carry down the aisle.

Bernt was the best man, Ivar and Karl were the groomsmen. Anna and Theodora stood up for Debra. The wedding went off without a hitch. All their friends and acquaintances were there. It was a big event. Everybody had a great time. Anna and Harold hosted a nice bridal dinner.

The newlyweds took care of lots of awkwardness after the wedding by surprising everyone when they left on a short honeymoon on the evening train going all the way to Fargo and staying in a hotel there for two nights.

Debra's parents went home Monday night. They concluded they preferred living in their comfortable home in Minnesota but they would come back when there were grandchildren to meet. Her mother was a bit startled by it all but was very happy because her "old maid" daughter was now the wife of a rich, hardworking farmer.

While they were on the honeymoon, the brothers and the other men got together and found another empty homestead shack nearby and bought it for a few dollars. They pulled it over on the snow and nailed it on the other side of the new kitchen addition as the master bedroom. The women cleaned it out. They cleaned up the old iron bedstead and bought a new mattress in town. It was their wedding present to the couple. The honeymooners were thrilled when they came home to what their family and friends had done for them.

#

Debra and Lars got to know each other and found more and more to agree about. The following August they welcomed their first child, a sweet baby girl they named Kristina. In less than a year they had met, got married, had a baby, and somewhere in between, fell in love. Lars was totally amazed and enthralled with his new wife and little daughter.

Living with a new baby and a newly married couple placed a strain on the three bachelor brothers. A baby crying at night greatly disrupted their sleep. It made them wonder if married life with kids was all it was cracked up to be. Their old bachelor life certainly had some advantages. On the other hand, they loved the better food, fresh baked bread every week, and having their clothes washed and pressed regularly. On the not-so-good side was those stinky diapers.

In the spring, they learned another neighbor had sold his land and there was a decent sized homesteader shack on it, complete with kitchen and such which the new owner did not need. After a quick discussion, Karl, Bernt, and Ivar made an offer on the shack. With a little bargaining, they made the deal. That night at the supper table they announced that they had bought themselves a separate house. Harold and Debra were surprised but not at all opposed to the idea.

The next day the men took three teams of workhorses to the claim. It was early enough in the season that the grain fields hadn't been planted and the pastures and hayfields hadn't grown much yet. They used shovels and pry bars to break the shack loose from the stone foundation. They found that once they got it moving, the horses didn't have that much trouble pulling it. The bachelor farmer helped them move it. He helped them take down two sections of barbed wire fence along their path and fixed his fences as soon as they were through and traveling on their own land.

The Johnsons had to take down a few of their own fences as they went. It took most of the morning to get it into their farmyard. They situated it on the opposite side of the yard, hopefully far enough away to not hear the baby crying. As they pulled it, they argued about the advantages of digging a cellar and putting their shack on top of it. They decided they were too busy right now with spring's work to dig a cellar. They used some of the abundant rocks to build a foundation under the shack and took great pains to get the whole thing leveled.

Debra inspected the dwelling as soon as they had it in place. It was dirty but seemed to be sound otherwise. Before the three men moved in, she spent two days cleaning and scrubbing the place top to bottom. She tried out the coal heater which worked well. This shack did not have separate rooms but that was no problem for the brothers. They put their beds in opposite corners, with the table and chairs next to the stove in the other. They had shared a bed since they were little. As young children, it was not unusual to have four or five in one bed. It was just the way it was with limited space. It also helped to keep them warm. The new shack wasn't very big but it would work because Debra said they would still eat all their meals in the main house. Karl tried to hurry the process by suggesting that she didn't have to scrub everything with lye soap water.

"If you think my baby is going to crawl around on your dirty floor, you can think again!" she retorted.

"Why would the baby be on our floor?" Bernt asked cautiously.

"You will babysit sometimes when I am real busy or have to go someplace."

"Where would that be?"

"Maybe to the church in town to get the baby baptized."

"She's already baptized, isn't she," Ivar asked, looking at the tiny red-haired girl.

"That one is," Debra said with a smirk. "But this one isn't yet." She put her hand on her tummy and that was how the boys learned another baby was coming. They looked at each other and had the same thought: *good thing we're getting out of the main house.*

#

As soon as Debra mopped the floor the second time, they barely let it dry before moving in their beds and the extra old chairs. They were not so concerned with how it looked as long as it was comfortable, warm, and, most of all, quiet. They were also looking forward to staying up late talking and laughing loudly without disturbing the baby.

Lars immediately noticed that Debra relaxed a bit more without the constant presence of his three brothers. She liked them, but living with them all under one roof was wearing on her. When she relaxed some, so did Lars. Now they could latch the door at night and pull the curtains.

Privacy was a luxury. They could walk around in their night clothes and Debra could take a bath near the warm stove without having to shoo the boys outside and having to rush. The next year they added a wash house where they had a coal stove and tubs for baths and washing clothes. There was more room there to hang up wet laundry to dry in the heated room. They made do with very little at first but kept adding more as time and opportunity allowed.

CHAPTER 15
Manfred Chooses a Bride

Manfred continued to make improvements on his farm. He built a two-roomed wood shack with a wood-shingled roof. Life in a soddie was fine for a while but it made him happy to have clean wood floors and a shingled roof, plus he knew no new wife would want to live in a soddie. He dug a basement with stacked rock walls and an outside hatch for a root cellar.

Besides that, he continued to improve his English and was writing to each of the three girls he met at the Grange Hall dance in Minnesota. He was very unsure of getting it right so he had Miss Sorenson help him. She was bemused to see him romancing three women by railroad mail. He got at least one letter back every week.

Over the winter he knew he would have to make a choice and struggled greatly with it. He talked about it with Anna and Theodora, then with Debra when the men weren't around. They asked him a lot of questions but were careful not to tell him who he should choose.

What he did not know was there had been several letters going back and forth from these wives to the girls' mothers back home trying to find a suitable match for him. Their mothers knew what the attitude of the girls were from their coffee klatches. All the mothers back home had been shocked by Debra's running away and getting married within weeks. They did agree that Debra would not have been a suitable wife for Manfred. After all, their daughters were much better catches.

#

Back in Minnesota, Betsy found herself being wooed by a railroad track man right there in town. He was a promising prospect. She heard all the gossip about Jane, Frieda, and herself throwing themselves brazenly at that North Dakota farmer. She was eager to end that speculation so when her new beau proposed, she accepted. She wrote a nice letter to Manfred about being engaged so he wouldn't be hearing from her anymore.

It was a gentle Dear John letter if there ever was such a thing. Manfred was not upset because it was one less woman to consider. He was not sure about the other two, after all he had only spent a few hours with each of them. They were lovely young ladies, terrific dancers, had nice parents, and cooked even better than his own mother.

When spring's work was done and the hay wasn't ready yet, Oskar said, "Time to go see Hilda and those other fillies." Manfred nodded. "Tomorrow night, the eleven-thirty train. Bring your nice duds. Who knows when you might need them." Manfred nodded again with thoughts mostly on seeing his beloved mare Hilda.

The next night they boarded the passenger carriage and tried to sleep in the hard seats. Oskar's Uncle John picked them up late the next night. They went right to Oskar's parents' house and hit the hay. Morning came real early with sunrise before five o'clock. At the horse barn, they checked the mares and new foals.

Manfred was delighted that Hilda had dropped another big strong colt. She recognized him and came to nuzzle him followed by her curious colt.

"She's a good mother. Breeds good, too," John said. "She has a lot of years and foals in her yet."

Manfred nodded, "She is happy and her scars are better."

"We put salve on them every week and keep socks on her legs most of the year."

"*Danke* for taking good care of her. I'd like one of her foals sometime." They moved on to check the rest of the foals and brood mares. Oskar had five new horses he had bought or traded.

"I think these can go up for farm animals," Oskar said. "They're all about three years old, prime stock, and strong." They examined them closely.

"Three mares, one gelding, and the gray one is a stallion," Uncle John said. "Do you know of anyone up there who could handle him? We don't have time to castrate him if you want to take him up there now."

Manfred said, "I know a strong farmer who could handle this stallion."

"Are you sure? Who?"

"Me!"

"Yup, that'd be a good match. Two studs on the same farm," Oskar joked.

John chuckled, "Better get some fillies then, too."

"How much?" Manfred asked.

"Mares should fetch about sixty-five each and seventy for the gelding."

"How much for stallion," Manfred asked, worrying if he could afford it or not.

Taking a deep breath, John said, "Oh, how about ten dollars and you give up your rights on Hilda?"

"I have rights on Hilda?" John nodded. Manfred put out his hand and they shook on it as Manfred added, "Including a rig big enough for him."

John rolled his eyes and laughed, "Why the hell not?" They all smiled and headed for the house for noon dinner where the talk was all about horse trading.

Ma spoke up, "You all get washed up in time to go to the Grange Hall at five o'clock. There's a meatball dinner tonight." The men nodded.

"Me, too?" John asked.

"You'd better show up. Your missus is bringing meatballs and gravy."

They worked on getting the horses ready to transport and drove them over to the railroad stockyard, ready to load that night at eleven o'clock. They had brought the tarp and heavy quilt even though it was summer. The nights would be cold.

#

When they returned, they washed up and dressed in their good clothes. At the hall, Oskar seemed to find a lot of old friends so Manfred was kind of abandoned. "Heard you were back in town," a sweet voice said behind him. "Were you going to come a calling?"

Manfred turned around and saw Frieda Morgenstern. He gave her a big smile and said, "Yes, I was hoping tonight but we have been busy with horse buying every minute."

"Is that the only reason you came back?" she said looking at him slightly askance.

"No, the main reason was to see you."

"Just me? You know Betsy got married on Sunday."

He nodded. "Hope she got a good husband. She's nice."

"Yes, she did and she is," Frieda said as she took him by the hand and led him into the line for the meatball smorgasbord. As they dished up, he took extra when she pointed out the meatballs and gravy she had contributed. There was a small table off by itself that she steered him to. They talked as they ate. There was an unasked question that went unanswered as they caught up on each other's news.

She liked hearing about his new two-room house and was delighted to get all the details about Debra, her husband, the baby, and another on the way. She laughed and laughed. "Debra was never one to ask permission for anything," she said. "I guess she hasn't changed."

Manfred was very nervous because he didn't want to spoil the evening if the marriage question came up. They stayed undisturbed until eight o'clock when dinner was over and Frieda had to go in the back to wash dishes. She pulled him into the coat closet for a moment. Looking him in the eye, she said, "I'm still interested." She gave him a warm kiss that lasted until they heard someone coming, then she turned and ran into the kitchen.

Still somewhat shocked, Manfred just stood there until he heard Oskar say, "Thought I'd better rescue you before she had you roped and branded." Manfred exhaled loudly. When they went out to the surrey, Oskar pushed Manfred away and said, "You ride in that buggy."

There sat Jane Larsen. He walked over and she said, "Get in. We'll take the long way home. I know you have to leave soon."

As he climbed aboard, he said, "I was going to come see you."

With a pleased smile, she said, "Well, now you don't have to. I'm here." She drove the horse, steering the carriage around the other wagons and horses easily. Manfred thought she was a good horse driver. "I'm glad you liked my food basket last time," Jane said with a flirty glance.

"*Wunderbar*, delicious. Again, I thank you."

"I saw you eating and talking with Frieda." When Manfred didn't answer, she said, "We're good friends you know."

Not meeting her eyes, he replied, "No, I did not know that."

"We read each other's letters from you."

Manfred nearly fell out of the surrey. "*Mein Gott* (my God)! I hope I didn't make you mad or anything."

Jane laughed, "If either of us was mad do you think we would have shown up here tonight?" Manfred sat there at a real loss for words and she asked, "Cat got your tongue?"

"Cat? What cat? I don't know this?"

"Just saying I would like to hear what you're thinking."

"Maybe I go back and save stamps. Write one letter to you and Frieda together."

"Oh, I don't think that's a good idea." She stopped the buggy near the trees in front of Oskar's folks' place. Turning to him she said, "Does this mean Frieda and I have to keep chasing you? We don't want to have to fight over you." He looked her in the eye but kept silent. "We won't wait forever. Betsy gave up and got a good man already. Debra's mother is calling us old maids."

"I like you both. I don't blame you if you run away from such a *dumkopf* as me."

"Here comes Oskar, I think he's eager to get on the train." She put her arms around his neck and gave him a kiss, then another, and then a long, warm one. "Get out," she said, giving him a little shove. "And take that," she said pointing to a basket of food. He got out without conscious thought and she drove away fast while he stood gazing at the retreating buggy, basket in hand.

"Thought I had to rescue you again before you got branded twice," Oskar said with laugh They went in to change into their work clothes and pack their bags.

"Manfred, if you're going to keep coming back here and courting those girls you could just as well leave that good outfit here," Ma said mischievously.

They said their thank yous and goodbyes. Pa drove them to the train where he helped wrestle the horses into the slat-sided cattle car. It took all three of them to force the stallion in. He wanted nothing to do with this strange smelling, noisy contraption. Finally, they put a shirt over his eyes and pulled him as he snorted.

By the time they got the horses tied up, they had to make their own sleeping nest with the tarp and quilt after the train pulled out, blowing its whistle in a cloud of steam. It was a long trip, not getting in until a day-and-a-half later because of track work. They talked about horses and crops but steered clear of anything about women even though Manfred couldn't think of anything else.

#

Two weeks later, Harold sent Anders over to Manfred's with an invitation to noon dinner at Lars and Debra's. Manfred never turned down a home-cooked meal. He rode with Oskar, Theodora, and baby Kristina.

When they went in the house, everyone was lined up looking at Manfred. To his utter shock, there stood Frieda and Jane. "Thought I'd invite my friends for a visit," Debra said. "Sit down. Time to eat." Stunned, Manfred was seated between the two single women. Mortified, he was still not ready to choose. A dull red crept up his neck.

Manfred didn't eat as much as he usually did, and was unnaturally silent throughout the meal. When they finished eating, the women went to deal with the babies and talk about womanly things with the single girls.

The men were herded outside to look at the bachelors' bunkhouse as they had started calling it. "Nice," was all Manfred could muster up.

Bernt and Ivar said almost together, "Are you a *dumkopf*? Why do you dither? If you wait another day, we will marry those beauties ourselves and you'll keep sleeping in a cold bed."

Manfred was trapped but knew they meant it. They were his friends but jealous of his choices. The girls had come by train the day before and would leave on the evening train in two days.

After some cajoling and arrangements by the wives, each girl would go to spend an afternoon on Manfred's farm. Oskar or Harold would go along and stay in the background just in case. No one wanted any rumors flying about Manfred entertaining unescorted women. They drew straws to see who went first. It went as you might imagine. Manfred was nervous as a cat in a kennel of bulldogs. The girls were single-minded in their determination.

When the evening came for them to leave on the train, Manfred was at the depot and so were all the Johnson brothers and Debra. Debra spent some time whispering to Manfred and then gave him a shove.

"Manfred has an announcement!" she shouted. That shut everyone up as they froze in place.

#

Twisting his hat in his hands, Manfred said, "I do not know how this is properly done." He glanced at Debra who nodded encouragement. "Frieda, you appear to like my farm better and my cows liked your hand at milking. I like that we can speak German together. If you would marry me, I would be greatly honored."

Frieda and Jane both burst into tears and hugged each other, not him. Finally, Jane said, "You better be good to her mister, she's my best friend." He nodded dumbly. "If you don't, I'll come up here with Grandma's rolling pin and pound knobs on your head." He didn't doubt it for a minute.

Bernt stepped up carrying the girls' bags because the train was almost ready to pull out. The locomotive blew its whistle and the conductor yelled, "All a-board!"

"Kiss her you idiot," Ivar yelled over the noise which spurred Manfred to hug Frieda and give her a quick kiss.

Frieda beamed at him. "I have to go home now but I'll write and we can make wedding plans." The girls got on the train with Bernt carrying their bags. He whispered something to each of them before jumping off the train as it jerked to a start.
Everybody waved.

When the train was gone, the wives hugged Manfred, and the men shook his hand offering congratulations. His life was never the same after that. He sent Frieda a nice letter that he rewrote three times with the help of Miss Sorenson. It was his formal proposal of marriage and a future life together. His letter crossed in the mail with one Frieda had sent accepting his train platform proposal. She was thrilled and said many times that Jane was happy for the both of them. She said her parents were excited for her and couldn't wait for the wedding to take place.

The wedding was arranged for two weeks later. They couldn't delay because harvest would start right after that. Manfred agreed to go to Frieda's family's church in Tranquil for the wedding. Two days before the wedding, the men had a bachelor's party in North Dakota. Lots of beer and even a bottle of German Schnapps were enjoyed. Manfred got pretty drunk and was singing, laughing, and dancing. All the men were more than a little drunk. The next noon when they loaded Oskar and Manfred on the train for Minnesota, they still looked a little green around the gills.

Everyone was surprised when Bernt and Ivar got on the train with them, carrying their best clothes packed in Debra's travel case. They refused to miss their good friend's wedding. Besides that, they had an ulterior motive: bridesmaids. Nobody else could afford the tickets or the time away from summer work to go.

When they arrived, Pa picked them up. Ma was very happy that Manfred was finally going to marry a local girl. She eyeballed the Johnson boys, already trying to figure out a match for them.

The wedding came off nicely. There was dinner after and a wedding dance that the bride and groom had to leave halfway through to catch the night train for two days of honeymooning in the big city of Minneapolis.

The Johnson brothers were not good dancers like Manfred but they never sat out a tune. The only time they had a break for a beer was when the band did. The two handsome bachelors left a rosy glow on many a woman's face that night.

When it came time to leave the next night, Bernt made a startling announcement. He wasn't going back. He was staying right here and he'd find a job here.

Ivar half-shouted, "Did a horse kick you in the head? What are you trying to do? Lars is going to be furious. We have crops to harvest!"

Bernt refused to get on the train with Ivar and Oskar. He cashed in his ticket and asked Ma if he could rent a room. She smiled and said, "Of course."

The train pulled out without him.

#

When they got home, Lars was incensed that his brother would desert them right at harvest. "He ain't getting no cut of this harvest. He screwed us! Goddammit!" He stomped away and no one dared say a word.

The wives were full of questions about the details of the wedding and where the newlyweds were honeymooning and for how long. Some far-fetched guesses and stories went around. The next night, Manfred and Frieda came in on the train. They had many trunks and boxes of her things and gifts from family and neighbors. Frieda had pretty much surveyed what Manfred had in his new two-room shack when she had spent the afternoon there, and what was still in the old soddie, so she brought what she knew she needed.

Kelly and Peggy happened to be in town picking up their mail when the train came in. They had heard of the wedding but hadn't even met Frieda yet. It was a fun meeting, with Frieda intrigued by the new O'Neal baby, a boy named Aidan who had red hair like his sister. They gave them a ride home in their wagon chatting all the way. Peggy was happier yet to have another woman in the area. She had been there when Debra delivered and knew her well from that. She speculated that it wouldn't be long before they'd be delivering another baby to the newlyweds.

Kelly helped Manfred hitch up his wagon to go right back to the depot and pick up their freight. Frieda was almost frantic to get started filling Manfred's shack with all her things and making it their home. They traveled together on the trail, stopping very briefly at Harold's to let them know the newlyweds were home.

Manfred drove them the rest of the way in and they loaded the wagon until the wheels creaked. They had to tie heavy rugs over the top. Manfred drove slowly so they didn't break the wagon's back or a wheel. The wheels were squealing by the time they pulled up to their door. They spent the rest of the day carrying everything in and unpacking. Manfred was busy putting legs on a new table and assembling her brass bedstead and the new mattress.

She had him lug in some shelves from the soddie and an extra bench from the barn.

When they were working hard later in the afternoon, Anders came walking over. His mother had told him to help with their milking and anything else they might need. He milked the cows and fed the horses like he'd been doing for the week Manfred was gone. He was shy around Frieda. She was a beauty and he was of an age where he was starting to realize the parts of marriage nobody talked about. He couldn't wait until he was old enough to marry. He thought Manfred was very lucky.

Frieda offered him some of the food her mother had sent with but he declined because his mom had said to be home for supper at seven o'clock. Frieda kept him busy with helping her make beds, unpack pots and pans, and bring coal in for the stove. He pumped some fresh water for the kettle. She liked this boy, growing fast into manhood. He was real awkward around her. Manfred thought it was funny. "He looks at you and walks into walls," he laughed.

#

They got most of the furniture set up by sundown. It had been a long day after a long night on the train. They were enthusiastic newlyweds and jumped in to initiate their new bed. After expressing their love a few times, they fell into exhausted slumber in each other's arms.

WHAM! BANG! Clank, bang, bang, "Yahoo" at their door. They had been sleeping maybe an hour. As they struggled awake, they saw lanterns outside, heard people singing, and children shouting. It was an old-fashioned shivaree. All the neighbors had gathered at Harold's farm and sneaked up close to Manfred's place where everybody could start pounding on the walls.

Frieda knew right away what it was, but Manfred had never heard of such a thing. Frieda reached out and grabbed her heavy flannel nightgown, slipping it on under the covers before jumping up waving to all the people crowded round looking in their windows and hollering. It was chaos. Frieda threw Manfred his trousers and held the blanket up so he could get them on in some modesty. Frieda laughed and smiled so he did, too.

They unlatched the door and the people poured in. They brought in tubs of homemade brew and lots of food. There were many slaps on their backs and hugs with introductions all around. Frieda grabbed her dress and headed to the outhouse to change while everyone hooted and hollered while making completely inappropriate comments. Double-entendres abounded even from the wives.

Frieda liked the beer and took all of the kidding with good humor. Manfred was not quite as sure of it all. "How often does this happen," he asked.

"Don't you worry, it's only one time for newlyweds," Oskar said. "We all had one but never this big."

"It's fun and brings good luck," Lars said, putting another jar of beer in Manfred's hand. The party kept going, singing, some dancing, two fiddles, and a washtub playing. The kids crapped out first and were laid on the bed and on the floor under coats while the grownups continued the shivaree until the crack of dawn.

Manfred and Frieda were almost dropping with exhaustion by the time they were abandoned with shouts of: "Don't do anything we wouldn't do" and singing "Hot Time in the Old Shack Tonight." They looked to see if any kids had been forgotten. None had been, so they latched the door with a chair propped against it for extra security.

Without any more thought, they dropped their clothes, and climbed into bed to get some sleep. They slept soundly for a few hours when they heard Anders and Johan shout. "We did the milking. Ma says you should stay in bed." So, they rolled over and slept some more. About noon they got up, still suffering from lack of sleep, too much noise and celebration through the night.

"Good morning, Missus," Manfred whispered to his bride. "Welcome to your new home."

"Good morning, Mister," Frieda smiled tenderly. "Welcome to *our* new home. I was going to make you a big breakfast early this morning but something happened."

"It was good? Ya?" Manfred asked just to be sure.

"Only good friends and neighbors throw shivarees. It's very good," Frieda said with a reassuring look."

They took it easy the rest of the day doing light chores, milking cows, and putting more things away. Pictures of her grandparents were hung on the wall as were some of Frieda's fine needlework pieces. One fine oil painting, a landscape of the Alps in the moonlight, was carefully placed away from the stove where everyone would see it. They fried eggs and bacon for supper and went to bed as soon as the sun went down. After all they were newlyweds.

Their marriage was off to a great start. Life was good. Frieda liked their neighbors and they liked her, too. She fell asleep dreaming of things to come.

CHAPTER 16
Bountiful Harvest

Soon after the shivaree and settling down some, the
Eisenschmidtts got harvest season started in earnest. Everyone was
out cutting and tying the cut wheat and barley into bundles and
stacking them in shocks. The oats and rye could wait. Wheat and
barley were the cash crops that would make or break the farm. The
price of wheat spiked up because of a wheat failure in the Ukraine
and Germany, so it was in much demand to keep those populations
from starving.

When the shocking was done, they worked on the rye and then
on the oats. They needed to get the cutting done or the
grasshoppers could come in. Sometimes grasshoppers would just
eat a few leaves and move on. Other times they would strip a field
clear down to the dirt. Swarms of locusts could eat entire fields of
grain. Anders had hung his shirt on a fence post while he was
driving the horses with the harrow when a swarm came through.
When he got back, his shirt had been eaten. Nothing but the collar
and buttons remained. The hoppers even ate the bark off wood
fence posts. Rain drowned out most of the grasshoppers still in
their larvae pods.

Gardens would wait until the first frost. They had plenty of
hay this year, there were big haystacks all over the countryside. It

was good times for most of them. Failures happened, of course, mostly caused by inattention, lack of knowledge, or pure laziness of some not-so-good farmers. This was not a land where the lazy or ignorant thrived.

Wives worked in the harvest fields doing the cutting and binding along with any boy tall enough and any man young enough to tie them with a few lengths of straw. Some were fast and some learned to be fast but some never would catch on to it. Frieda proved to be hardy and quick, even as quick as Manfred. He had to work fast to keep up to her.

Whereas Lars's wife Debra was a town girl, she gave it a good try but it didn't come natural to her. They agreed most of her time was better spent keeping the three big men fed and clothed.

Peggy O'Neal was not very strong but she worked until Kelly made her quit. She was a good farmwife but couldn't do the hard labor. Everyone had their limitations but they always exceled at something. Farming was a family endeavor especially at harvest time. There was never any shortage of work.

One of the big problems they had this year was the railroad didn't have enough boxcars to haul the bountiful crops and there weren't enough bags or granaries to store it in. Some filled their barns or piled it up on high, dry ground and covered it the best they could with straw. Grain buyers always lowered the prices at harvest time because they knew most of the wheat had to be sold right then or risk it spoiling. Prices went up in the winter but it was harder to get it to market until the roads were covered in snow for the sledges.

The most astute farmers kept some of the best looking grain for seed the next spring or to sell to other farmers who might want a new strain.

When the farmers finally organized, they dealt with the railroads to build big grain elevators on railroad sidings. "Cathedrals of the Plains" they were called. They were what you saw on the horizons until the tree claims grew high enough to see from afar.

Each year seemed to bring something new. One fine fall day before noon, Harold was startled when a big work wagon with a windmill and tower on it pulled into their farmyard. Anna came out of the house just as the driver hollered, "Yo, Missus! Here I've got your windmill and pump. Where you want the well?"

"Anna?" Harold exclaimed, then said quietly, "What is this? I didn't order this."

"It's from money my uncle gave me in case I needed something. I've saved it long enough. We need it, Harold." To the driller she called, "We want it over there between the house, the soddie, and the barn."

The driller jumped down and pulling out a long Y-shaped willow twig. He held an end in each hand with the third end sticking straight out ahead of himself. He started walking around the area between the buildings.

"What's he doing?" Anders asked, mystified. All the children, who now numbered seven, watched him go back and forth.

"He's a water witch. He uses the willow stick to find the best water," Harold said.

Johan blurted out, "He's a witch? On our farm? Won't he eat the kids?"

"Oh for heaven's sake. He's not that kind of witch. He's a good sort of witch," Anna told them, but the little kids backed up and only peeked around the corners at the strange man with the stick. They had heard witch stories. They didn't know anything about good witches, just the ones who stole or ate children.

Suddenly, the end of the stick quivered and then pointed straight down when he took two more steps. He scratched an X in the ground and then spit a stream of tobacco juice dead center on it. "This be the best clear water," he announced. He looked at Anna for affirmation.

"Harold? Is that place good for you?" Anna asked. Harold was still shaking his head at the surprise and audacity of it all, and threw his hands up in resignation. Anna looked to the well driller and nodded. He pulled his wagon closer and tilted up a small wood trestle tower with a heavy iron pipe that stood exactly on the X. He hooked his horses to a long rope attached to a driving weight that started to slam the point of the pipe into the ground with a thump, thump, thump. The boys and little children watched in fascination.

"How deep you going?" Harold finally asked.

"Felt like about twenty-five foot but there be a bigger pool down about forty foot if'n you want it deeper. But that'd cost another, um, seven or eight dollars."

Anna said, "No, twenty-five feet will be just fine. All for the price I already paid."

"Yes Missus," he said as he kept driving the pipe down. When it was almost at ground level, he had the horses pull the driving weight to the top of the trestle and locked it up there. He unscrewed the driving cap, put it on another length of pipe, and screwed that one into the one in the ground. He started the horses pulling the driving rope again. He did that one more time when they could hear the *thump, thump, thump* change to more like a *squatch, squatch, squatch*, and when suddenly it was *thud, thud, thud*, the driller stopped.

"That be it," he announced. The pipe was about two feet above the ground where the driller unscrewed his driving cap. He used a fine brass chain to lower a long brass cylinder with a few little holes in the bottom and let it fall down the pipe. Anna and Harold heard a splash. The driller let the chain slowly slide a little deeper

213

and kept going about four more feet. "Good water pool," he announced, "five to six foot deep." He quickly pulled the chain up and looked at the water streaming out of the little holes while he held it up to the sun. Then he sniffed it with a nod and sipped from the stream. "Here, taste," he said, so Anna and Harold did. "It be good, sweet water. This be a good well for ya. You'll never pump this one dry even if you let the windmill pump all day all year long. It's worth every buck."

# # #

He pulled the steel windmill tower sections out of the wagon and bolted them together. Then he pinned two of the legs into the ground with plates and four-foot steel stakes. Harold held the windmill gear head in place while the driller bolted it on top and then attached the big blades in a circle around the hub.

"Easiest to bolt together on the ground," he said. "Don't have to lift those iron gears so far this way." He hooked his drive rope to the top of the windmill tower and to his horses. "Can you stop my horses when I yell whoa?" Harold nodded and held the team by their bridles. "GeeUp EeeeeZeeee," the driller called out. The horses had done this many times, so they slowly pulled as the top of the tower came up. The driller helped lift it at first, then it went up faster. When he hollered, "Whoa" the horses stopped mid-step, but Harold held them just the same. The tower settled upright with all four legs on the ground.

The driller pulled out two more big, steel shoe plates and bolted them to the legs, adjusting the level. Then he pounded more steel anchor pins through them. "Won't go no place now." He looked around and added, "Course if you piled some big boulders on top of the plates it'll keep the tornados from lifting it up."

He assembled the sucker valve and rod, lowering it down the hole to hear it splash and sink. Next he put the hand pump over it all and screwed it tight to the pipe. He pulled the sucker rod up about two feet and put in the keeper pin. "Give her a pump young man," he said to Anders as he pinned the pump handle in place.

Anders pumped but all it did was rattle at first before quieting down. "Can one of your kids bring out a coffee pot," the driller asked. Anna had Kersta run in for it. When she gave it to him, he hung it on the spout just as fresh water splashed into it. "That's enough boy," he said as the big, white, enameled metal pot filled. To Anna he said, "Can you make us a cup of coffee? Just to celebrate?"

The driller measured and hooked up the drive rod from the windmill gear box. "See if we got any Dakota wind today," he laughed. "It'll swivel so it points the blades into the wind all the time. Works like a weather vane, too." He pointed to Johan and Anders. "Here's the gear lever. Pull it down and the pump starts. Lift it up to stop it."

Anders, now fifteen and strong, went to the wood lever connected by a rod to the gear box above. He pulled it down with a clunk and they all watched as the blades started to spin in the wind and the drive rod went up and down. In a minute, water started to gush out of the spout.

"Now you lift it up," the driller said pointing to Johan. When it stopped, the driller looked somewhat proud. "You tell all your neighbors that you know the best well driller in the whole county. Course I'm the only one," he roared.

"You're going to have to get a spout pipe to go to your watering trough. Put it more than fifteen feet away or you'll have a mud bog here," he said as he walked over to his wagon and pulled out a fifteen-foot spout pipe designed to hook on the well spout. "It's three dollars but if that coffee's done, then I'll give it to you for a buck."

Anna said, "It's ready, but we'll drink it out here." She went in and brought out a cup of coffee for each of the grownups and the well driller. She put ten dimes in the driller's other hand, "Thank you, it looks like a good well."

"You will thank me every day that you don't have to pump it or fetch buckets."

"I'm sure you're right."

He loaded up his drive ropes and got the trestle tipped on the wagon again and drove away with a wave. Harold looked at the windmill pump and then at Anna. He smiled, "You're definitely the smart one here. We should've done this years ago. That hand-dug well was never very good." They ran the fill pipe to the water trough as the boys took turns pulling the lever up and down until the tank was almost overflowing. The cows and horses drank from the tank. It must have tasted better than the slough water they'd been drinking. Blondie stood on her hind legs to lap the fresh water. The ox couldn't seem to get enough at first.

#

The next years went by in much the same rhythm. People moved to homesteads, others left, children were born, raised, educated, and some became farmers themselves. The Krosses attended a one-room country school until they finished eighth grade. The law at that time was you had to complete eighth grade or attend until you were sixteen years old, whichever came first. It was considered a full education for working people.

Some kids might have gone to high school if they lived in town and if they didn't have so much work to do on the farm. Even in the shops in town child labor was common, and at the age of thirteen with an eighth-grade diploma, you qualified for most jobs except the military where a parent had to sign for you. The eighth-grade law stayed in effect until the mid-1960s.

The only organized sport for country boys was baseball. Most males, young and old, participated whenever they good. The town had a regular team that played for many decades.

Christmas seasons were joyous with so many families around. There were always house parties and big feasts. Presents were usually simple and useful, many of them homemade. Many a little girl was delighted to open her gift to find her old painted tin doll's head with a new, stuffed cloth body and a new dress cut from someone's worn out clothing.

Boys might get a new pair of overalls or a flannel shirt, not their most thrilling gifts, but they were taught to be thankful for everything. They all had one present under the tree from the parents and maybe one from the grandparents. They exchanged names in school for a gift but those were limited to nothing costing more than a nickel. It wasn't so much about the contents but more about the thrill of having a package to open.

Sunday school kids always performed a Christmas program for the families and grandparents who sat in rapt enjoyment watching the children. The teenagers would come marching in from the back of the darkened church carrying burning stubs of candles, hot wax dripping on their fingers as they tried to keep their flame going while singing. If someone's candle went out, a small titter would ripple through the kids. As soon as they were lined up facing the congregation they blew the candles out.

Under the tutelage of their Sunday school teachers, they would sing and say their memorized pieces and quotes from the Bible. The littlest kids were proud to sing in their high monotone voices and act out "This Little Light of Mine" and pretend to be looking for the Star of Bethlehem. People did not clap in church but oohed and aahed over the little ones.

After the prayer, everyone joined in for "Silent Night" and other popular Christmas songs. At the end of the program, kids were each given a small brown bag filled with candy: hard ribbon candy, black licorice, candy corn, peanuts in the shell, walnuts, Brazil nuts, chestnuts, and filled chocolate mounds, provided by the local merchants. Candy was a rarity for kids in those days, it was considered a waste of hard-earned money. The kids made a big deal of trading away the ones they didn't like to get the prized chocolates.

As with every community, not everyone was nice and honest. Older siblings picked on younger siblings, big kids picked on weak kids, sometimes physically but mostly mockery and name-calling. The teachers tried to keep the bullying down but it was a losing battle while teaching the three R's, geography, and penmanship to kids in eight different grades. Some teachers lasted a few years, some didn't last that long. They didn't go away in failure but usually succumbed to the courtship of a local bachelor leading to marriage and immediate dismissal.

#

Settlers had to be frugal so they reused, repaired, and patched everything they could for as long as they could. Patches on patches were normal. One neighbor who was very short in stature was not short on brains. He noticed that the denim overalls they all wore were the same price no matter the size, so he ordered his in extra-long. He bragged that he had an extra foot-and-a-half of denim free from each leg that he cut off and used for patches. Free was free so he was admired but also teased good-naturedly for his miserliness. The common attitude was to not spend hard-earned money needlessly. The phrase "waste not, want not" was often repeated.

Many an evening was spent darning socks. Heels and toes wore through fast trudging mile after mile behind the horse and ox teams in heavy farm boots. Field hands covered many miles every day, sometimes walking for twelve to sixteen hours. They were only limited by the durability of the horses and oxen. Many teams were switched out at noon for the heaviest work like plowing sod. Men and boys guiding the plow were expected to keep going. Even when socks were worn to a frazzle they would unwind the uppers to reclaim the yarn for darning. No wonder "darn it" was a curse.

Skills varied. A homesteader with blacksmithing equipment and skills could make more money doing repairs and equipment rebuilding than by farming. Those who had the knack and feel for farrier work were constantly in demand. People brought their lame horses with loose or missing horseshoes or sometimes the farrier would come to their farm. Horses were their most valuable resource and were happier and worked harder when well- shod.

Farmers sharpened their tools daily. Some were better at it than others but a sharp tool made for easier work. A sharp scythe cut swift and clean without wearing out the man swinging it. Picks, chisels, sickle blades were sharpened daily; shovels were sharpened when sod, outhouse holes, and graves had to be dug.

Digging graves was a grim obligation. Family and friends, and church congregations did it themselves. It was immediate work because the dead had to be buried within a few days because morticians and embalming were not common back then. Burials occurred on family farms and were often unmarked, especially for infant deaths. Graves had to be dug in the winter, too. When frost had driven four-feet deep, it was like digging rock. Many times they burned piles of coal to thaw the ground a few feet at a time. It was sad, grueling, but necessary labor.

One neighbor had grown up cutting trees in Norway and kept his saws and axes razor sharp. He worked them on a big sandstone sharpening wheel morning and night and carried an axman's sharpening stone in his overalls pocket. His reputation spread and soon all the ladies brought their good sewing scissors and shears only to him and the men brought their saws, too. Sharpening was a matter of pride and a skill passed down by hands-on teaching from generation to generation.

Every farmer had to have some butchering skills to make the right cuts for roasts and steaks. Skilled butchers traveled from farm to farm in the fall and winter. Meat grinders and sausage makers were essential to keep meat year around.

Many made their own beer based on long-used family recipes. It was a good way of preserving some of the grains. Germans called their heavy dark beer "liquid bread". It was more important to some than others. Most of the men and many of the women enjoyed a beer now and then. During harvest season, jugs of beer were kept in the water tank for a refreshing and revitalizing drink for the workers. Kids were not allowed to drink beer except for a sip now and then.

There were many who abhorred the use of any beer or hard alcohol because they had seen men destroyed by drunkenness. It was a common problem that never went away even during the years of prohibition when beer and booze were illegal. In fact, it flourished because farmers had the skills, the barley, and the place to make beer. Lots of money was made by some and spent to ruination by others.

Musicians of all sorts abounded. Brass bands, town bands, and orchestras were a great source of entertainment. Fiddle players and singers were common in many families, some good and some mediocre. Kids aspired to excel on some musical instrument or at singing. Soloists, duets, trios, and quartets competed with great pride.

By 1910, with the advent of the amazing Model T Ford car and truck, there was a thriving repair business because the heavy constant farm use and great travel distances wore out the engines, brakes, and transmissions.

CHAPTER 17
Harold gets a Daughter-in-Law

Typical of homesteader boys, Harold's oldest son Anders had been doing man's work since the age of nine, driving horses, harvesting, haying, and tending livestock. He gradually did heavier and more complicated work until there was no part of working a farm that he couldn't do. When he turned eighteen, he started farming his own land with horses and farm equipment that his father loaned him or lent him the money for.

Anders found a piece of land from a nearby failed homestead and moved into the two-room shack on his new farm. He was doing well but he was lonely there after four years of farming by himself. He did not want to be one of the sad, lonely bachelor farmers that were all too common then.

The main thing Anders desired and needed most to succeed in life was something increasingly rare out there. What he could not find was a wife. Younger single women wanted a more established husband while older or widowed women thought him much too young.

Trying to think of where he might find the ideal wife, he remembered back a dozen years to that last summer Bible school near Tranquil, Minnesota and his first little girlfriend, Sarah. It was farfetched but so far nothing else had worked in his romantic attempts, so why not? Maybe she'd remember him even though he'd never written to her since they'd left.

He was hesitant, but finally mentioned the idea to his mother. He was surprised how fast she encouraged him. Anna advised, "Anders, it's time you showed a little gumption if you want to get a girl's interest. I'll give you the penny for the stamp and help you write a nice letter."

Taking her advice, he wrote to Sarah Larson in Woburn, Iowa. He had nothing to lose. His mother asked if there were any other girls he wanted to write to but he didn't think so right now. He wrote the best letter he could and asked Oskar and Manfred for advice. They were surprised but they and their wives were happy to help. After many efforts, they came up with a nice, appropriate letter that he nervously sent by railroad mail.

Back in her Woburn, Iowa hometown for her mother's funeral half a century after she had started her westward journey, Sarah clearly remembered how her marriage to Anders had come about so fast. It was the turning point of her life. She could not have imagined what was going to come of it but even now it all seemed so improbable.

A very surprised but bemused Sarah was intrigued by an out-of-the blue letter from Anders Kross. She hadn't thought of him for years. Curious about life out on the prairie and what his intent was, she wrote back with lots of questions. She had heard stories of some young women from around Tranquil who had been romanced by rich young farmers from North Dakota a decade ago and had married happily as far as she knew.

With a little trepidation, her reply letter started a romance. The speed of their courtship was made possible by the swift railroad delivery of mail. A letter from Iowa to North Dakota would arrive in two to three days. Having a romance by rail-mail sounds strange to us now but it was not uncommon back then when there were no telephones or internet.

Unbeknownst to Anders, Sarah was not a novice to courtship letters because she was already having a rail-mail romance with Teddy, a family friend who had moved to Chicago a few years before. She now had two possible romances going, one east and one west. Being an old maid wasn't as much of a worry with all that attention. She was a busy girl writing to and being wooed by each man.

Although Anders had been her childhood crush, she was more intrigued by the successful Teddy in Chicago. She thought Teddy was hinting at a more serious relationship, hopefully even marriage.

Sometimes though, life throws you a curveball. With no forewarning, Teddy's letters stopped and when he did not reply to her following letters, she was puzzled and hurt. She felt no choice but to give up on him. Anders never knew that he'd had a courtship rival and their letters continued to flow.

Anders' mother hired a photographer to come and take pictures of the entire family on their farm and, most importantly, of Anders on his homestead. Weeks later when the pictures finally came back from the film lab, his mother helped him pick out the best ones to send to Sarah. The next time he wrote, he sent two pictures, one of him standing with his four work horses, wagon, three cows, and dog standing in front of his two-room home and the sod-walled barn.

The other picture was from his confirmation a few years before where he looked young, fit, and handsome. Sarah thought he had not changed much and wrote back saying how much she liked his pictures and his farm. Feeling more encouraged with each new letter from Sarah, after a few more weeks, Anders carefully wrote a letter proposing marriage, full of promises for a good life.

After the arrival of his proposal letter, Sarah was still torn between her fears of moving so far away to the unknowns of a Great Plains farm versus her dread of being an old maid. After asking her mother for advice, her mother reminded her that she herself was barely seventeen when she traveled across the ocean from Norway and halfway across America to end up marrying a much older man.

At least Sarah knew Anders from childhood and they had all heard about his father's very successful homestead. From the pictures he sent, it was obvious that he was doing well for himself. Even though her mother hated to see her go, she thought it could be a good match. There was not much else she could tell her.

#

Finally, after some sleepless nights, Sarah wrote a reply saying she would be happy to become his wife in North Dakota. In a few weeks, she had packed all she could in a few trunks with some family heirlooms and gifts from her widowed mother and sisters. They could not spare the money for train tickets to attend the wedding, so there were tearful family goodbyes at the depot. Sarah promised to come back to visit often. She boarded the train alone, going across the plains to begin married life on Anders' farm in northwestern North Dakota.

When the acceptance letter came, and in the weeks until Sarah came on the train, Anders was giddy with excitement. His family and friends were even happier that he had finally found a wife from a good farm family. When her train arrived, Anders and many of the family were there to greet and meet her.

He was pleased that she was still the sweet pretty girl he remembered, and she was pleased with him, too. She spent the first few nights at the home of his parents, Harold and Anna. They were all busy making food and getting the fixings and clothes ready for the happy occasion.

Sarah was just nineteen and Anders was all of twenty-three, a perfect time for married life to start in those days. Some wondered why they had waited so long. The wedding took place in the church parlor in Northfield, with just the minister and Anders' parents as witnesses. They went right to a wedding celebration at his parents' farm.

All his family and their friends were there to celebrate and bestow their blessings upon them as well as giving the young couple many useful gifts. The slightly used brass washboard, stoneware dishes and cups, and a good old butter churn were well received. Anders' cousin Snowball splurged on a new cotton-filled mattress from the Sears Roebuck catalog for them that arrived in a freight car just in time for the wedding.

A neighbor lady had made a big, white, wedding cake, and others contributed their specialty foods for an enormous feast. They danced to the lively tunes of the fiddle and accordion players, and plenty of their best home-brew was enjoyed. Everyone made their best efforts to have a good time.

There was way too much drinking after the wedding for Sarah's comfort. It was not something she was used to, but she painted a stiff smile on her face and kept quiet about it.

They did not go away for a honeymoon because it was October and there was still more hay to put up and gardens to be harvested before winter set in.

She knew the rural traditions for newlyweds so when the shivaree crowd came calling in the middle of their second night, she at least had a robe and slippers handy. She went along with it and Anders had a great time. The neighbors, friends, and families stayed and partied, drinking beer, eating, and singing until dawn. It was exhausting but fun for all, even the newlyweds.

#

They newlyweds settled down and Sarah immediately set about turning the little frame house into a home more to her liking. It felt drafty from the first night, so she spent a lot of time chinking cracks and weather-stripping door and windows. She cleaned the iron cook stove and tested its oven. Anders had to buy a few pieces of stovepipe so they wouldn't be smoked out when winter and snows came.

Sarah had lived in a sturdy, nicely finished farm house that her father had built up until now. She wanted those same comforts in her own home and made sure Anders knew he should help her make it so. He loved her all the more for it.

Sarah found she had to do lots of other farm chores and hard work that she'd always thought was men's work. She and Anders worked day and night to build up their farm. She never complained to him, but confided in letters to her mother that Dakota farm life was much harsher than she was used to.

The winters were long, windy, and cold with so much snow that they were often isolated for days or weeks at a time. Anders had brought in enough coal so they could keep warm and she could cook.

While they did get plenty of snow and wind, there were always stretches of milder winter weather with brilliant sunshine and blue skies. Everyone celebrated by visiting and hosting neighbors. They were not working sixteen-hour days like in the spring and summer. It was a fun time making new friends of the family and neighbors around them.

They minded their stock, and milked the cows, and appreciated the modern cream separator they received as a wedding gift. All Sarah had to do was turn the handle fast enough and long enough for the flywheel to make the regulator start to *ding, ding, ding*, signaling it was ready for her to pour the raw milk into the big top kettle. Metal discs inside separated the skim milk and rich, fresh cream.

The cream went into two containers. There were always separate cream cans for fresh and sour cream. Skim milk was used for cooking, drinking, and feeding the calves and pigs. They always had too much cream even though they used plenty on their daily oatmeal and for baking. They kept some fresh cream on hand but mostly they saved up big cans of sour cream that they sold at the train depot for railroad shipment to a big creamery. Cream checks were like a gift and usually used for luxuries or other necessities.

Sarah made lots of rich, salted, sour cream butter that they used for cooking, frying, and on bread. Smaller amounts of unsalted, sweet cream butter were made and used for baking fine pastries and cakes. Sour cream was used on potatoes and many exotic Scandinavian baked goods and desserts. The milk from a cow's first milking after having a calf was sweet and rich enough that when baked, made a wonderful flavorful pudding.

One of the Norwegian neighbor's wives made cheese from cow's milk and goat's milk. There was a type of cheese their own family made from culture they used year to year. There was another exotic type of cheese that they missed here. It wasn't a cheese culture that anyone here had and when her neighbors' sisters in Norway tried to mail her a piece to act as a starter culture for it here, the customs agents seized it because it was not on the approved import list.

The sisters in Norway tried again by dipping a piece of rough cloth in the cheese culture when it was still liquid. They dried it carefully and sealed it in waxed paper in a mail envelope. It got past the customs agents and came through. The neighbor woman was able to use it and made that cheese for many decades. It was a favorite specialty cheese appreciated by some but not all.

A big pot of cottage cheese was always on the back burner of the range. They ate it straight and used it to make other cheeses. One type of cheese that was either loved or hated was *gammel-ost* which literally translates to "old cheese". They made it pretty wet and put it in an old sock to hang out on the porch to cure. The kids all said it smelled like dirty socks but the grandparents especially loved it.

Refrigeration was not yet available on the farms. The creamery in town did have a frozen locker plant because they needed to keep milk cold for shipment. Some people rented a frozen locker to store their meat in before the days of home freezers. Some people had ice houses if there was a place to harvest ice blocks in the winter.

A common and relished form of preserving was slicing thin pieces of beef and drying it in the sun with salt. They pickled pork and pigs' feet. Some of their cash went to buy pickled herring, salt cod, sardines, and lutefisk for Christmas. It was typically only served when they had guests. Some neighbors from the south and east were aghast at those treats. Some choked it down but just as many refused to taste it. Food was how the society expressed its togetherness and love.

###

Sarah and Anders worked hard for the good life and their first baby, a son, arrived the day before Thanksgiving of the following year. The next baby was a girl, and a year-and-a-half later, a son was born who lived only a few days.

Sorrow took its toll but four more healthy children put Sarah through all the trials of motherhood. She raised them with the support of Anders' family but sorely regretted her children not knowing their maternal grandmother and aunts.

The population of Wesley County peaked in 1905 with all the new settlers on their homesteaded claims. Slowly the number of people dwindled as more families sold or abandoned their farms. Some moved to town or to larger cities. Towns grew when farm families moved in.

Not all years were good. Not enough rain or killing frosts destroyed crops and gardens. The price of grain kept steadily declining and railroads kept increasing freight rates because there were no alternatives to move grain to markets, mills, and shipping ports. At that time, it cost more to ship a bushel of wheat to Duluth, Minnesota than it did to ship it from Duluth to anyplace in Europe or Asia.

Big bankers colluded to impose outlandish interest rates and land seizure policies to the detriment of the settlers. Even so, the area became more settled and improved. Some roads were being built at the expense of higher taxes. Many immigrants and homesteaders could not or did not know how to pay all the taxes on their land.

Railroads were the only way to bring in merchandize and carry all their grain and animals to markets far away. Sometimes a boxcar full of seasonal fruits or bulk goods would arrive. When fresh apples came in, they were bought by the bushel for next year's pies and cider. Boxcars from the south brought in crates of peaches and pears. Barrels of raisins, prunes, and dried apricots from California came in, and peanuts by the bushel sack were always a treat. Sealed boxcars filled with sacks of white flour, white sugar, and boxes of salt were always in demand. Molasses by the barrel was prized. Refrigerated cars delivered fish, fruit, and fresh vegetables. Settlers had to be quick if they wanted to get bulk goods because they sold out fast. If merchants bought it all up settlers would end up paying higher prices.

Mail orders from catalogs arrived steadily and provided a variety of goods and tools not available any other way. Regular mail service from the railroad depot to other cities was fast and efficient. The Post Office sorted mail in special cars as the trains were on the move. Letters could be mailed in North Dakota and delivered within two days in Minnesota and letters from coast to coast made it in four or five days. Business was fast and efficient largely because of fast mail.

Railroad passenger service became cheaper and more comfortable. Luxurious Pullman sleeping cars, quality dining cars, and better passenger seats made travel not only easier but downright fun. It was the best way to see the countryside, natural wonders, awe-inspiring parks, and vistas.

Locomotive engineer was the dream job for boys in the days of fast, powerful, steaming, smoking engines pulling enormous trains of cars at incredibly fast speeds.

CHAPTER 18
Life Goes On

After some hard years of establishing their family and farm, Anders and Sarah were startled by a declaration of war against Germany by the United States. The President had promised to never go to war.

Many farmers were drafted but some did not have to go if they were the only man with a family on the farm. A lot of bachelor farmers were drafted to fight in the trenches in France against the German army. Many were killed or wounded and almost all of them were gassed to some degree. They hated the gas most of all. For the most part, folks who homesteaded had gone to America to get away from wars, armies, and other countries' wars. They served now because they had to but they felt they had been lied to by the President that they had elected.

One of Sarah and Anders neighbors was sent to fight in the War to End All Wars. They invited him to dinner now and then and he told his war story often. "I come from Ukraine, I speak only German," he said. "I homestead, I speak only German. My horses understand only German."

Shaking his head, he said, "American Army send me letter. I go to Army, I don't speak English, only German. They put me on big ship, send me to France war against Germans. They march me into trenches, I still speak only German."

"I holler, '*Wo bist du! Actung!*' Germans shoot at me, French shoot at me, English shoot at me, even Americans shoot at me." He coughed, "Just one night was I in war trench. Then they make me a cook. Too dangerous for them to have me in war." He laughed and said, "Didn't want to kill nobody, never shot one time."

He was a nice man, a gentle soul. A decade later he died of lung problems because even the cooks got exposed to mustard and chlorine gas during that war.

#

The years after the war were prosperous. Wheat prices peaked at the end of the war but steadily dropped over the next decade to half of what it had been. Even so, there was money to be made by good farmers who had not gone into debt.

Prohibition came, so there were plenty of illegal transactions for beer and liquor and smuggling across the nearby Canadian border. Some watched boats and barges full of Canadian whiskey silently slink down the lake from Canada on moonless nights.

Border Patrol agents used big mirrors to look under cars and trucks for prohibited liquor. The border itself was too long and too open to patrol effectively. Some regularly crossed into Canada via prairie trails to attend church services and social events because it was closer than going into their own town. Small town church basement lutefisk and lefse winter dinners were attended by hundreds.

Elections were held at country schools. The Parent Teacher Organization (PTO) held monthly meetings which were attended by even the bachelors because it was their tax money helping to support the schools. They held card parties and whist tournaments there that were hotly contested. Soft-spoken, mild-mannered men were seen standing up at the tables shouting and shaking their fingers at other usually mild-mannered friends. Uffda! But again, the entertainment and lunches were good.

Their woodchopper neighbor who sharpened scissors had a funny falsetto voice. At some of the gatherings he would roll up his pantlegs, wrap a towel around his waist, use a dishtowel for a headscarf, and climb up on a table to sing and act like a silly girl. His wife was mortified but he laughed and so did everyone else. He ended his routine by playing his violin and many got up to dance. People had to make their own entertainment in those days.

The somewhat timid storekeeper's wife would do readings, switching her voice for all the characters to the delight of the kids and neighbors. She would scurry off the stage to the thunderous applause.

School meetings followed Roberts Rules of Order and voting rules, an education in American democracy for young and old together. There was no American royalty to tell them what they had to do like in the countries they had emigrated from.

#

Anders and Sarah's tidy farm did quite well until the 1929 stock market crash which started the Great Depression. The local bank failed and they lost their savings and seed money. It was just gone, and no way to get any of it back. Many felt that the government let banks steal from the common man.

On top of that, the Dirty Thirties drought hit hard. Sloughs and lakes dried up completely and they saw the bottoms were covered with buffalo bones. Hayracks full of bones were sold at the railroad siding for shipment to fertilizer plants back east. It was a little extra money when they needed every penny. Many arrowheads and stone tomahawks were discovered in the fields after the wind blew the dirt away exposing them.

The drought left them without anything to harvest or hay for the livestock so farm life became impossible. They had no cash for taxes and nothing left to sell.

Anders' father had lost almost everything, too, and was barely able to hang onto his own farm. He wanted to help Anders and Sarah but had nothing left to do it with. Farms were failing and being auctioned off by the banks and tax collectors. They kept hoping and praying that next year the rains would come back so they could survive these terrible times. The harder it got, the more desperate and discouraged they became.

Drought killed the wheat, and the grass dried up, so the soil blew away in great dark clouds from horizon to horizon blocking out the sun sometimes even in the middle of the day. It was so dark they had to light lanterns in the house. The sugar bowl and flour containers were wrapped with cloth or the fine dust got into them. Ponds and shallow wells went dry so they had to give up or pay the driller to go deeper.

Cattle and horses were starving so the government bought them up at a pittance only to shoot them on the spot and burn them so no one could have the meat.

County Agents advised farmers to chop the only thing growing in the fields, Russian thistle, while it was still green, and feed their stock on it through the winter. It allowed the cattle to lose weight slower because they had a four-stomach digestive system that could almost handle it, but horses sickened and died when they tried to eat it. Many lost all of their horses.

Some tried to plow using Model T cars and others invested in one of the little gasoline tractors. At least tractors could sit without being fed and they could still be sold if need be.

Those who could save their best horses were proud of their bloodlines winning blue ribbons at the county fairs. Anders' pair of

Belgians were so well-matched that the fair judges couldn't say which one was the best.

Schools and churches were kept open with teachers accepting county scrip in place of money, and preachers had to settle for bread and chickens instead of cash in the offering plates.

More and more people pulled up stakes and headed for promises elsewhere. Most of the advertised jobs were hyped up to lure families and when they arrived, no work was available and conditions were worse than where they came from.

The government started the Civilian Conservation Corps (CCC) and the Works Progress Administration (WPA) work programs for boys and young men and directed most of their pay back to their families. It saved many a farm from auction.

People needed entertainment, more than ever before. Town bands and marching bands were found in towns large and small. Early radios started to link remote farms to the rest of the nation. News and weather forecasts became instantaneous. The President went on the radio to tell them they didn't have anything to fear but fear itself. A memorable statement but it didn't save anybody.

The local men's baseball team was good and played other towns and semi-pro teams. Anders was the star pitcher and his cousin Snowball was the catcher. In 1935, they played the Bismarck semi-pro team and faced Satchel Paige, a big man from the Negro Baseball Leagues who went on to the Major Leagues in 1948.

In the end, Anders and Sarah, like tens of thousands of farmers from Texas way up into Canada, lost their farm. Except for the youngest daughter, their other children were mostly grown and had to find their own work during that terrible time.

With no other options, they left on the train through the mountains to Oregon. At last, with some luck and perseverance, Anders started a part-time job with a village street department that turned into full-time work. He worked his way up to supervisor which allowed him to provide for his family again.

After a half-decade there, they scrimped and saved enough to buy a modest home. Mother Nature beat them down again when the raging Columbia River broke the Vanport dam. A fast flood swept away their house and everything they had. They barely escaped with their daughter and themselves.

From then on, they had a tougher go of it, never again able to make enough for the better life they had created and lost twice over. Anders could only find low-paying jobs in the sawmills where the work was tough and dirty.

It distressed Sarah greatly as Anders relied more and more on alcohol to blunt the pains of life's disappointments. He would work all day but went from work to the taverns for the rest of the night.

Sarah was alone except for the daughter who still lived at home. She did what she could, but it took its toll on her as well. She no longer had the support system of farm neighbors and relatives that she yearned for.

# # #

In spite of everything, Sarah managed to tuck away a little here and there out of the grocery money Anders gave her each week. When the telegram came about the passing of her ninety-five-year-old mother, she took the money she had hoarded to buy a round trip train ticket to Woburn, Iowa for the funeral. Anders could not go with because he had to keep working to pay the rent.

It was a hard thing for Sarah to come home to Iowa half-a-century after having left her family. With raising children, busy farm work, and never a spare dime for a vacation, she had never been able to fulfill her promise to come back to see them. Sarah's guilt about that and the grief of her mother's passing weighed heavily on her because she was now a grandmother in her seventies without many rewards for a hard-worked life.

As the train neared town, she took in the lush countryside. Almost in a daze, she stepped off the train into the welcoming arms of her sisters and cousins. She went with her sister Mathilda to freshen up. Their brother Harry and his wife Ethel had come in the night before from western North Dakota. The viewing was that evening and the funeral was to be the next day at eleven o' clock.

It was not a surprise that Mother had passed on but it was still a sad time for them. This gathering was to show respect and remember her. It was hard to see her in a coffin. "She looks so small," Sarah said.

"She always was small. Imagine Mother coming here from Norway at seventeen to help her cousin Elsa, Father's first wife, with their six children only to have Elsa die shortly after. Mother married Father and outlived him by sixty-five years. Less than ten years later, he died and left her with eleven children and one on the way," Thelma said.

"We come from hearty stock. At least on Mother's side," Mathilda said. "Glad we picked the right one to take after."

"Mathilda, stop joking, our dear Mother just passed."

Many distant family members came for the viewing. There were nieces and nephews and their children who she had only seen in a photo now and then. They were anxious to meet their long missing Great Aunt. Many of them remarked, "You look just like Mathilda" to which they replied, "We'd better, we're sisters."

"She wanted to see you again so bad," Thelma said, causing tears to spring to Sarah's eyes again. "But she understood why you couldn't come back. We didn't get hurt by the Depression and Dirty Thirties like you did."

"We're the four she didn't outlive. There aren't many who live that long and she never lost her sharpness," Mathilda said.

Sarah felt good to be back home with her sisters and brother. She quickly embraced the pleasure and comfort of her own family, and the laughter that she had been missing.

The funeral was held in the old country church which Father helped build in the 1870s. It was filled to standing room only. Mother's funeral was more of a celebration of life than a time of sorrow. The way it should be.

Great-grandsons bore her coffin out to the church's cemetery where she was buried beside her long-departed husband. It was somber and dignified. Sarah was saddened that her mother was never able to go back to Norway to see her family either.

Lunch was served in the church basement by the Ladies Aide. It was crowded and many came to talk to them. They welcomed Sarah back with open arms, making her feel loved and safe. Hours later when the last ones left, they were on the brink of exhaustion. They went to Mathilda's for a quiet supper and spent the evening together talking.

Sarah, Mathilda, and Thelma felt the decades melt away. The next morning, they visited the old family farm, remembering the vigorous healthy life their family had. They laughed about playing blindman's bluff in the house with the lamps off, and of the fun they had playing kick-the-can or tag or hide-and-seek in the farmyard. The old farm had changed with the new occupants but it was mostly the same for them. The landscape and the sounds in the little valley were calming.

#

Since they saw Harry and Ethel off on the afternoon train and it was mild weather for December, the sisters stayed downtown. Arm-in-arm they strolled one familiar street after another looking at the homes and businesses, talking nonstop trying to fill in what they had missed of each other's lives. It was a joy for them to just be sisters again. They went to a church basement dinner and the service afterward.

When they left, feeling peace and contentment, they were confronted with that serendipitous moment that only happens in real life. Coming out of the church right behind them, who should they run into but the other man: Teddy, the rail-mail romancer who spurned Sarah fifty years ago.

They stopped dead, staring as they recognized each other. Politely, though a bit stiffly, they chatted with him. He had come back to town to spend a week with his family for Christmas.

"I heard of your mother's passing but could not there in time for the funeral," Teddy said. "I am sorry for your loss, my sincere condolences."

They chatted a bit more not knowing what more to say after the polite platitudes. When Teddy revealed he had never married,

Sarah was unable to contain herself and blurted out, "Then why did you stop writing?"

Visibly startled, Teddy sputtered, "I, I didn't stop writing. You did!"

Bewildered, Sarah shot back, "I sent many letters after your last one. Didn't you get them?"

"Oh, Sarah," a quavery-voiced Mathilda confessed, "it's my fault! I liked Anders better then Teddy, so I tore up the letters you were sending to each other."

Speechless with outrage, Sarah glared at her sister. Stepping between them, Thelma tried to make peace by apologizing, "Teddy, Sarah, I'm so sorry! I didn't know. Mathilda had no right to interfere in your lives like that back then. She was just a foolish girl."

Teddy and Sarah looked from Mathilda to each other in shock. The stunned old man stammered sadly, "Oh Sarah, what a life we might have had." He turned, tears in his eyes, walking away to his Cadillac at the curb.

Sarah was left awhirl, wondering how different her life might have been with Teddy, who was driving out of her life again. Furious, she left abruptly on the night train, never to return. Thelma tried in vain to patch things up between the sisters, but even she couldn't undo the life-altering betrayal. Sarah never again talked to nor forgave Mathilda.

#

It was a long, tearful, three-day train ride across the country back to Portland and her meager home there. When Sarah stepped off the train, Anders was bewildered at her angry sadness and aloofness.

He thought she was grieving for her mother, but it never went away. He dared not ask about her anger every time she tore up letters from one of her sisters. He wondered what could have happened to take the spirit out of his wife but she would not let him ask.

They quietly lived out the rest of their lives together, for in those days, once you married it was for better or for worse - until death they did part.

End

Dedication

To my sister, Gloria Opseth Ryberg, my excellent editor, without whose encouragement, organizational skills, constancy, and sharp eyes, my novel could not exist.

To my brave frontier homesteader families who broke the prairie and established a solid thriving rural society out of the emptiness that was the Great Plains.

Also to my family who taught me the art of storytelling and creative imagination, my teachers, and family who fostered my love of reading and books, and to the rural frontier society and those old settlers whose tales of endurance inspire me.

About the Author

Larry Odin Opseth is a retired architect, watercolor artist, and a true bibliophile. He is also a storyteller, writer, student of history, and a collector of personal life stories.

Born at the end of WWII, he grew up on a North Dakota farm homesteaded by his Norwegian grandparents. His heritage is of immigrant homesteaders, who valued storytelling, active conversation, colorful imagination, and hard work.

One of his illustrated Norwegian Folktales stories has been published in the Historical Press of Norway.

Educated in small North Dakota schools, he worked his way through a Bachelor of Architecture degree at NDSU, and became a licensed Architect.

He delights in the anomalies of history not easily found in common history books.

NOVELS BY THIS AUTHOR

Available on Amazon.com

NOTCH-EARED PONIES - Breaking Mustangs in the Old West

The wild west frontier was not a kind or gentle place for people or horses. This short story is an excerpted part of my two yet unpublished books about the end of the Civil War and the drive west by war's survivors. It is based on the lives and work of cowboys and ranch widows who embarked on an all-or-nothing cattle drive after the war. They were battle-fatigued survivors from the Civil War. As mixed a group as could be found: Yankees, Rebels, militia, men, and boys who somehow lived while every other man in their units was killed. They chose to drive a cattle herd west with their Osage Confederate scout guiding them through the wilds of the Texas range lands. With winter approaching, they settled into an abandoned ranch. To their surprise, they found three ranch widows living nearby. There was civility to be relearned by these scarred men of war who had long before left behind families and women. They celebrated the winter and were joined by an ancient ranch man and his teenaged orphan granddaughter. In the spring they started rounding up the scattered longhorns that had gone wild during the war. They decided to stay together and drive the cattle across Texas, west around the Indian Territory, and east through Kansas to the railhead at Abilene where the Texan beeves were worth more. The group had only a few genuine cowboys amongst them. Most had everything to learn about becoming drovers of the roughest stock in the west. The ranch widows, adapted to this life, helped them learn on the trail. From the start it was obvious they had too few cowponies. They were desperate to increase their remuda so they could put enough asses in the saddles to make the cattle drive a success. They traded with the Indians for a bunch of wild mustangs with notched ears that had to be broken. This was not gentle training or Horse Whisperer or My Little Flicka horse breaking. This was flat out wild west rodeo bronc busting. It had to be done without breaking the men while subduing the wild ponies. This is the wild west that old-time cowboys would recognize. It may seem to be a brutal story but it was the reality of surviving in the last half of the 1860s.

HOMESTEADERS HOPES - Taming the Wild Prairie

Homesteading the unbroken buffalo grass Great Plains in the late 1800s wasn't for the weak or fainthearted. Settlers like my grandparents arrived with little more than hope and the promise of free land. They fought snow, forty degrees below zero temperatures, and blizzards that lasted for days. They suffered through the summer heat, untimely droughts, prairie fires, grasshoppers, exploitation by the railroads and the crooked politicians. Homesteaders came from all over including the flood of European Immigrants. They set up their own society with the strangers who happened to homestead next to them. Working together was essential for survival. Many of them failed or died trying. These were hard working folk who knew if they failed they could starve and lose everything. Theirs are the stories that were repeated by the thousand-fold. Those Homesteaders were hardworking, determined people who had successes and failures and endured the Great Depression and the dust bowl of the Dirty Thirties that forever changed the landscape of that rural society. Many of my family and friends will recognize some of the people, places, and stories in this novel even though I have changed the names and places to protect their privacy.

Spirits Series:

1 - **LOST SPIRITS OF THE CIVIL WAR** - Remnants of War

None of them were singing the "Battle Hymn of the Republic" or "Dixie" even though their shooting war had been halted. They were starved, exhausted, more dead than alive. They had appeared out of nowhere for us to save fifty years ago. My men thought they might be the ghost spirits of soldiers who suffered through the war. The 150th anniversary of the Civil War and the 100th anniversary of World War I are upon us. This novel contains soldier survivors' stories of both wars. The veterans of those wars have now passed on, but their experiences still hold lessons for us all. The Civil War aka War Between the States aka War of Secession was the bloodiest American war ever. One character in this book is a veteran of the War to End All Wars, now known as World War I.

2 - **YOUNG SPIRITS** - Seeking General Lee

What do two frontier kids do when the Confederate Army steals their Pa while they are out fishing? They hitch up their pony cart and go searching for him, of course. Josie was only 13 and Aksel 10, but they were quite self-reliant and used to doing for themselves on their Missouri farm. Their Ma died 4 years ago and now Pa was gone too. They were determined to seek out General Robert E. Lee to ask if Pa could go home with them. It was a perilous journey, the Confederates and the Union armies were battling throughout their travels. They stumbled upon the remains of battles and horrifically wounded soldiers. Their Pa had taught them to never let anyone or anything suffer, so it was pure instinct for them to help. They bandaged soldiers using strips of their own clothing and saved as many as they could. They wintered with war-torn families who offered to take them in permanently but they were determined to find their Pa. Because they were children, soldiers, officers, and Generals from both sides tried to send them to somewhere away from the war but did help them however they could. They didn't know it was an adventure. To them it was simply staying alive and trying to get Pa back against all odds. They grew up beyond their youth in the 2 desperate years of searching.

3 - **WANDERING SPIRITS** - Wrangling West

The American Civil war is over. The Confederacy has surrendered, and its armies disbanded. Lincoln has been assassinated. The Federal Army is rushing in to occupy all the unconquered parts of the south. The slaves are freed but along with the war-ravaged southerners have few choices of where to go and little ability to provide for themselves. The soldiers of the Federal Army want to go home but their leaders need them for the occupation of the yet defiant southern states. A group of starving, hopeless survivors of both sides' armies are saved by the generosity of a young Lieutenant's supply fort in southwestern Missouri. These men rightfully fear the coming of the occupation army so they escape further west. They start a life of survival and hope along with a few ranch widow women survivors from the emptied ranchlands of Texas. Together they struggle, traveling and working together, while seeking some place of prosperity and peace. They have too few horses, too few experienced cowhands and way too many wild longhorns but they try a trail drive across Texas, around what will be Oklahoma and back across Kansas to the Abilene railhead to sell them. They encounter tragedies and bad luck but they keep going the best they can.

4 - **WESTWARD SPIRITS** - Rails and Trails

Here we are on the edge of the big North and Western Railroad camp, ready to start another venture. But why not? We've been soldiers from both sides armies in the Civil War, ranchers for a winter in Texas with resilient ranch widows, cowboys on a longhorn cattle drive all the way from Texas to Abilene, Kansas, and now a company work gang on the transcontinental railroad. We've somehow survived Civil War battles, starvation, rescue, war fatigue, and hard losses on the cattle drive. We are learning how to be a bit more civilized and even joyful sometimes, under the strict tutelage of those wonderful ranch widows and other characters who have joined us along the way. Now we have become the Blue and Gray Company, and I've found myself the Major in charge of everything, promoted under the orders from Bernice, Arne's new old wife. We have some cattle money in our pockets and the promise of profitable work on the railroad, even though there undoubtedly will be more losses and hardship. Who knows what will follow. Maybe we'll keep going westward until we find someplace to settle in peace with families for the good life that we've been yearning for.

Emma Series:

1 - **EMMAS MAGIC AXE** - Mystical Ancient Finds

2 - **EMMAS STOLEN AXE** - Twice Taken

3 - **EMMA GOES VIRAL** - Under Northern Lights

4 - **EMMAS LOKI TRICK** - Who's the Sly One?

Please Post Book Reviews on Amazon

Comments Welcome by emailing: larryopseth@msn.com

Made in the USA
Columbia, SC
04 May 2019